VAMPIRE BREATH

Look for more Goosebumps books
by R. L. Stine:
(see back of book for a complete listing)

#10 The Ghost Next Door
#11 The Haunted Mask
#12 Be Careful What You Wish For . . .
#13 Piano Lessons Can Be Murder
#14 The Werewolf of Fever Swamp
#15 You Can't Scare Me!
#16 One Day at HorrorLand
#17 Why I'm Afraid of Bees
#18 Monster Blood II
#19 Deep Trouble
#20 The Scarecrow Walks at Midnight
#21 Go Eat Worms!
#22 Ghost Beach
#23 Return of the Mummy
#24 Phantom of the Auditorium
#25 Attack of the Mutant
#26 My Hairiest Adventure
#27 A Night in Terror Tower
#28 The Cuckoo Clock of Doom
#29 Monster Blood III
#30 It Came From Beneath the Sink!
#31 Night of the Living Dummy II
#32 The Barking Ghost
#33 The Horror at Camp Jellyjam
#34 Revenge of the Lawn Gnomes
#35 A Shocker on Shock Street
#36 The Haunted Mask II
#37 The Headless Ghost
#38 The Abominable Snowman of Pasadena
#39 How I Got My Shrunken Head
#40 Night of the Living Dummy III
#41 Bad Hare Day
#42 Egg Monsters From Mars
#43 The Beast From the East
#44 Say Cheese and Die — Again!
#45 Ghost Camp
#46 How to Kill a Monster
#47 Legend of the Lost Legend
#48 Attack of the Jack-o'-Lanterns

Goosebumps®

VAMPIRE BREATH

R.L. STINE

SCHOLASTIC INC.
New York Toronto London Auckland Sydney

A PARACHUTE PRESS BOOK

ISBN 0-590-56886-8

12 11 10 9 8 7 6 5 4 3 2 1 6 7 8 9/9 0 1/0

Printed in the U.S.A. 40

First Scholastic printing, November 1996

"When a werewolf creeps up behind you at night, he steps so silently you can't hear a thing. You don't know the werewolf is there until you feel his hot, sour breath on the back of your neck."

I leaned over and blew a big blast of hot air onto the back of Tyler Brown's neck. The kid's eyes bulged out and he made a sick, choking sound.

I love baby-sitting for Tyler. He scares so easily.

"The werewolf's breath freezes you so you can't move," I said in a whisper. "You can't run away. You can't kick your legs or move your arms. That makes it easy for the werewolf to rip your skin off."

I sent another hot blast of werewolf breath onto Tyler's neck. I could see him shiver. He made a soft whimpering noise.

"Stop it, Freddy. You're really scaring him!" my friend Cara Simonetti scolded me. She flashed me a stern scowl from the chair across the room.

Tyler and I were on the couch. I sat real close to him so I could whisper and scare him good.

"Freddy — he's only six," Cara reminded me. "Look at him. He's shaking all over."

"He loves it," I told her. I turned back to Tyler. "When you are out late at night, and you feel the hot werewolf breath on the back of your neck — don't turn around," I whispered. "Don't turn around. Don't let him know that you see him — because that's when he'll *attack*!"

I shouted the word *attack*. And then I leaped on Tyler and began tickling him with both hands as hard as I could.

He let out a shout. He was crying and laughing at the same time.

I tickled him until he couldn't breathe. Then I stopped. I'm a very good baby-sitter. I always know when to stop tickling.

Cara climbed to her feet. She grabbed me by the shoulders and tugged me away from Tyler. "He's only six, Freddy!" she repeated.

I grabbed Cara, wrestled her to the floor, and started tickling her. "The werewolf *attacks again*!" I shouted. I tossed back my head in an evil laugh.

Wrestling with Cara is always a big mistake. She punched me in the stomach, so hard I saw stars. Really. Red and yellow stars. I rolled away, gasping for air.

Did you ever have the breath knocked out of

you? It's not a good feeling. You really think you'll never breathe again.

Making me see stars is Cara's hobby. She does it all the time. She can do it with one punch.

Cara is tough.

That's why she's my best friend. We're both tough. When the going gets tough, we never crumble!

Ask anyone. Freddy Martinez and Cara Simonetti. Two tough kids.

A lot of people think we're brother and sister. I guess it's because we look a little alike. We're both pretty big for twelve. She's an inch taller, but I'm catching up. We both have wavy black hair, dark eyes, and round faces.

We've been friends ever since I beat her up in fourth grade. She tells everyone that *she* beat *me* up in fourth grade.

No way.

Want to know how tough we are? We *like* it when our teacher squeaks the chalk against the chalkboard!

That's tough.

Anyway, Tyler lives across the street from me. Whenever I baby-sit for him, I call Cara, and she usually comes along. Tyler likes Cara better than me. She always calms him down after I tell him stories to scare him to death.

"It's a full moon tonight, Tyler," I said, leaning close to him on the green leather couch in his den.

"Did you look out the window? Did you see the full moon?"

Tyler shook his head. He scratched one side of his short, blond hair.

His blue eyes were wide. He was waiting for the rest of the werewolf story.

I leaned closer and lowered my voice. "When a werewolf steps out under the full moon, hair starts to grow on his face," I told him. "His teeth grow longer and longer, and pointier. They don't stop until they reach under his chin. Fur covers his body like a wolf. And claws grow out from his fingers."

I raked my fingernails down the front of Tyler's T-shirt. He gasped.

"You're really scaring him," Cara warned. "He isn't going to sleep at all tonight."

I ignored her. "And then the werewolf starts to walk," I whispered, leaning over Tyler. "The werewolf walks through the forest, searching for a victim. Searching . . . hungry . . . walking . . . walking . . ."

I heard the footsteps in the living room. Heavy footsteps thudding over the rug.

At first I thought I was imagining them.

But Tyler heard them, too.

"Walking . . . walking . . ." I whispered.

Tyler's mouth dropped open.

The heavy footsteps thudded closer.

Cara turned in her chair to the doorway.

Tyler swallowed hard.
We all heard them now.
The heavy, thudding footsteps.
"*A real one!*" I shrieked. "*It's a real werewolf!*"
All three of us screamed.

2

"Give me a break," the werewolf said.

Of course it wasn't a real werewolf. It was Tyler's dad.

"What are the three of you doing?" Mr. Brown asked, pulling off his overcoat. He had blond hair and blue eyes like Tyler.

"Scaring Tyler to death," Cara told him.

He rolled his eyes. "Didn't you do that *last* time?"

"We do it every time," I replied. "Tyler loves it." I patted the kid on the back. "You love it — right?"

"I guess," he said in a tiny voice.

Tyler's mom stepped into the room, straightening her sweater. "Were you telling werewolf stories to Tyler again, Freddy?" she demanded. "Last time, he had nightmares all night."

"No, I didn't!" Tyler protested.

Mrs. Brown *tsk-tsked*. Mr. Brown handed Cara and me each a five-dollar bill. "Thanks for baby-sitting. Do you want me to walk you home?"

"No way," I replied. Did he think I was some kind of wimp? "It's just across the street."

Cara and I said good night to the Browns. I didn't really feel like going home yet. So I walked Cara home. She lives on the next block.

The full moon shone down on us. It appeared to follow us as we walked, floating low over the dark houses.

We laughed about my werewolf story. And we laughed about how scared it made Tyler.

We didn't know that it would be *our turn* to be scared next.

Really scared.

Saturday afternoon, Cara came over. We hurried down to my basement to play air hockey.

A few years ago, my parents cleaned the basement up and turned it into a great playroom. We have a full-sized pool table and a beautiful, old jukebox down there. Mom and Dad filled the jukebox with old rock-and-roll records.

Last Christmas, they bought me an air hockey game. A big, table-sized one.

Cara and I have some major hockey battles. We spend hours slapping the plastic puck back and forth at each other. We really get into it.

Our air hockey games usually end in wrestling matches. Just like real hockey games on TV!

We leaned over the air hockey game and started to warm up, shoving the puck slowly back and forth across the table. Not trying to score.

"Where are your parents?" Cara asked.

I shrugged. "Beats me."

She narrowed her eyes at me. "You don't know where they went? Didn't they leave you a note or something?"

I made a face at her. "They go out a lot."

"Probably to get away from *you*!" Cara exclaimed. She laughed.

I had just come from karate class. I stepped around the hockey table and made a few karate moves on her. One of my kicks accidentally landed on the back of her ankle.

"Hey — !" she cried angrily. "Freddy — you jerk!"

When she bent over to rub her ankle, I shoved her into the wall. I meant it as a joke.

I was just goofing. But I guess I don't know my own strength.

She lost her balance and slammed hard into an antique china cabinet filled with old dishes. The dishes rattled and shook. But nothing broke.

I laughed. I knew that Cara wasn't really hurt.

I reached out to help pull her off the front of the cabinet. But she let out a roar of attack — and came hurtling into me.

Her shoulder caught me in the chest. I uttered a hoarse choking sound. Once again, I saw stars.

While I gasped for air, she grabbed the hockey puck off the game table. She pulled her hand back to heave it at me.

But I wrapped my hand around hers and struggled to wrestle the puck away.

We were laughing. But this was a pretty serious fight.

Don't get me wrong. Cara and I do this all the time. Especially when my parents are out.

I pulled the puck from her hand — and it went flying across the room. With a loud karate cry, I swung free of her.

We were both laughing so hard, we could barely move. But Cara took a running start and plowed into me once again.

This time she sent me sailing back . . . back. I lost my balance. My hands shot up as I crashed into the side of the tall china cabinet.

"Whooooa!"

I landed hard. My back smashed into the wooden cabinet's side.

And the whole cabinet toppled over!

I heard the crash of broken plates.

A second later, I fell on top of the cabinet, sprawling helplessly on my back.

"Ohhhh." My cry turned to a painful moan.

Then silence.

I just lay there on top of the fallen cabinet, like a turtle on its back. My hands and legs thrashed the air. My whole body hurt.

"Uh-oh."

That's all I heard Cara say.

A simple "Uh-oh."

And then she hurried over. She reached down, grabbed my hands, and tugged me to my feet.

We both stepped away from the fallen cabinet.

"Sorry," Cara murmured. "I didn't mean to do that."

"I know," I said. I swallowed hard, rubbing my aching shoulder. "I think we're in major trouble."

We both turned to check out the damage.

And we both cried out in surprise when we saw what the old wooden cabinet had been hiding.

3

"A secret doorway!" I cried excitedly.

We stared at the door. It was made of smooth, dark wood. The doorknob was covered with a thick layer of dust.

I had no idea there was a door back there. And I was pretty sure that Mom and Dad didn't know about it, either.

Cara and I stepped up to the doorway. I rubbed my hand over the doorknob, wiping away some of the dust.

"Where does this lead?" Cara asked, smoothing her black hair back off her face.

I shrugged. "Beats me. Maybe it's a closet or something. Mom and Dad never mentioned another room down here."

I knocked on the door with my fist. "Anyone in there?" I called.

Cara laughed. "Wouldn't you be surprised if someone answered you!" she exclaimed.

I laughed, too. It was a pretty funny idea.

"Why would someone hide the door behind a cabinet?" Cara asked. "It doesn't make any sense."

"Maybe there's pirate treasure hidden back there," I said. "Maybe there's a room filled with gold coins."

Cara rolled her eyes. "That's really lame," she muttered. "Pirates in the middle of Ohio?"

Cara turned the knob and tried to tug open the door.

I guess some kids would hesitate. Some kids probably wouldn't be so eager to pull open a mysterious, hidden door in their basement. Some kids might be a little afraid.

But not Cara and me.

We're not wimps. We don't think about danger.

We're tough.

The door didn't open.

"Is it locked?" I asked her.

She shook her head. "No. The cabinet is blocking the way."

The cabinet lay on its side in front of the door. We both grabbed hold of it. Cara took the top. I took the bottom.

It was heavier than I thought. Mainly because of all the broken dishes inside. But we pushed it and pulled it, and slid it away from the doorway.

"Okay," Cara said, wiping her hands off on the legs of her jeans.

"Okay," I repeated. "Let's check it out."

The doorknob felt cool in my hand. I turned it and pulled open the wooden door.

The door moved slowly. It was heavy, and the rusted hinges made an eerie *squeeeeeeak squeeeeeeak* as I strained to open it.

Then, standing close together, Cara and I leaned into the doorway and peered inside.

4

I expected to find a room in there. A storage room or an old furnace room. Some old houses — like my aunt Harriet's — have coal rooms where coal was stored to feed the furnace.

But that's not what we saw.

Squinting into total darkness, I realized I was staring into a tunnel.

A dark tunnel.

I reached out and touched the wall. Stone. Cold stone. Cold and damp.

"We need flashlights," Cara said softly.

I rubbed the cold, damp stone again. Then I turned to Cara. "You mean we're going into the tunnel?" I asked.

Silly question. Of *course* we were going into the tunnel. If you find a hidden tunnel in your basement, what do you do?

You don't stand around at the entrance and wonder about it. You *explore* it.

She followed me over to my dad's workbench. I

started pulling open drawers, searching for flashlights.

"Where could that tunnel lead?" Cara asked, frowning thoughtfully. "Maybe it goes to the house next door. Maybe it connects the two houses together."

"There *is* no house next door on that side," I reminded her. "It's an empty lot. It's been empty for as long as I've been living here."

"Well, it *has* to lead somewhere," she replied. "You can't just have a tunnel that goes nowhere."

"Good thinking," I replied sarcastically.

She shoved me.

I shoved her back.

Then I spotted a plastic flashlight at the bottom of a tool drawer. Cara and I both grabbed for it at the same time. We had another battle, a short one this time. I wrestled the flashlight away from her.

"What's the big idea?" she demanded.

"I saw this one first," I said. "Get your own."

A few seconds later, she found another flashlight on a shelf above the workbench. She tested it by shining it in my eyes till I screamed at her.

"Okay. Ready," she said.

We hurried back to the door, our flashlight beams criss-crossing each other over the basement floor. I stopped at the open door and shot the light into the tunnel.

Cara's light bounced off the stone walls. They

were covered with a layer of green moss. On the smooth stone floor, small puddles of water glimmered in the darting rays of our flashlights.

"Damp in there," I murmured. I took a step into the tunnel, moving my light along the walls. The air instantly felt colder. I shivered, startled by the change in temperature.

"Brrrr," Cara agreed. "It's like a freezer in here."

I raised my light and aimed it straight ahead. "I can't see where the tunnel ends," I said. "It could stretch on for miles and miles!"

"Only one way to find out," Cara replied. She raised her light and blinded me with it once again. "Ha-ha! Gotcha!"

"Not funny!" I protested. I beamed my light into her eyes. We had a short flashlight battle. Neither of us won. Now we both had bright yellow spots in our eyes.

I turned back into the tunnel. "Helll-looooooooooo!" I shouted. My voice echoed again and again. "Annnnnnybody hommmmmmmme?" I called.

Cara shoved me against the damp stone wall. "Shut up, Freddy. Why can't you get serious?"

"I *am* serious," I told her. "Come on. Let's go." I bumped her with my shoulder. I wanted to knock her into the wall. But her feet were planted hard. She didn't budge.

I lowered my light to the floor so we could see

where we were walking. Cara kept her light aimed straight ahead.

We made our way slowly, stepping around puddles. The air grew even colder as we walked deeper into the passageway.

Our shoes made soft, scraping sounds. The sounds echoed eerily off the stone walls. After about a minute, I turned back and glanced to the basement doorway. It was a narrow rectangle of yellow light, very far away.

The tunnel curved, and the stone walls appeared to close in on us. I felt a shiver of fear, but I shook it away.

Nothing to be afraid of, I told myself. It's just an old, empty tunnel.

"This is so weird," Cara murmured. "Where can it lead?"

"We must be under the empty lot next door," I guessed. "But why would someone build a tunnel under an empty lot?"

Cara raised the flashlight to my face. She grabbed my shoulder to stop me. "Want to turn back?"

"Of course not," I shot back.

"I don't, either," she said quickly. "I just wanted to see if *you* wanted to."

Our lights played over the damp stone walls as we followed the curve of the tunnel. We leaped over a wide puddle of water that covered the entire tunnel floor.

Then the tunnel curved one more time. And a door came into view.

Another dark wood door.

Our flashlight beams slid up and down the door as we hurried up to it. "Hello, in there!" I called. "Hellllooooo!" I pounded on the door.

No reply.

I grabbed the doorknob.

Cara held me back again. "What if your parents get home?" she asked. "They'll be really worried. They won't know where you are."

"Well, if they come down to the basement, they'll see the cabinet on the floor," I replied. "And they'll see the open door that leads into the tunnel. They'll figure out what happened. And they'll probably follow us in here."

"Probably," Cara agreed.

"We've got to see what's on the other side of this door," I said eagerly. I turned the knob and pulled the door open. This door was heavy, too. And it creaked eerily as it opened, just like the first door.

We raised our flashlights and sent our pale beams of light ahead of us.

"It's a room!" I whispered. "A room at the end of the tunnel!"

Our lights danced over the smooth, dark walls. Bare walls.

We stepped side by side into the small, square room.

"What's the big deal? It's empty," Cara said. "It's just an empty room."

"No, it isn't," I replied softly.

I aimed my flashlight at a large object on the floor in the middle of the room.

We both stared straight ahead at it. Stared at it in silence.

"What is it?" Cara demanded finally.

"A coffin," I replied.

5

I felt my heart skip a beat.

I wasn't scared. But my body started to tingle all over. A cold tingling. Excitement, I guess.

Cara and I both aimed our flashlight beams at the coffin in the middle of the floor. The light circles bounced up and down over the dark wood. Our hands were shaking.

"I've never seen a coffin before," Cara murmured.

"Neither have I," I confessed. "Except on TV."

The light reflected off the polished wood. I saw brass handles at both ends of the long box.

"What if there is a dead person inside it?" Cara asked in a tiny voice.

My heart leaped again. My skin tingled even colder.

"I don't know," I whispered. "Who would be buried in a secret room under my house?"

I raised my light and swept it around the room. Four bare walls. Smooth and gray. No windows.

No closet. The one and only door led back into the tunnel.

A hidden room at the end of a twisting tunnel. A coffin in a hidden, underground room . . .

"I'm sure Mom and Dad don't know anything about this," I told Cara. I took a deep breath and made my way closer to the coffin.

"Where are you going?" Cara demanded sharply. She hung back near the open doorway.

"Let's check it out," I replied, ignoring my pounding heart. "Let's take a look inside."

"Whoa!" Cara cried. "I . . . uh . . . I don't think we should."

I turned back to her. The light from my flash-light caught her face. I saw her chin quiver. Her dark eyes narrowed at the coffin.

"You're afraid?" I demanded. I couldn't keep a grin from spreading over my face. Cara afraid of something? This was a moment to remember!

"No way!" she insisted. "I'm not afraid. But I think maybe we should get your parents."

"Why?" I asked. "Why do we need my parents around to open up an old coffin?"

I kept the light on her face. I saw her chin quiver again.

"Because you don't just go around opening coffins," she replied. She crossed her arms tightly in front of her.

"Well . . . if you won't help me, I'll do it myself," I declared. I turned to the coffin and brushed my hand over the lid. The polished wood felt smooth and cool.

"No — wait!" Cara cried. She hurried up beside me. "I'm not scared. But . . . this could be a big mistake."

"You're scared," I told her. "You're scared big time."

"I am not!" she insisted.

"I saw your chin tremble. Twice," I told her.

"So?"

"So you're scared."

"No way." She let out a disgusted sigh. "Here. I'll prove it to you."

She handed me her flashlight. Then she grabbed the coffin lid with both hands and started to lift it open.

"Whoa. It's really heavy," she groaned. "Help me."

A shiver ran down my back.

I shook it off and set the flashlights down on the floor. Then I placed both hands on the coffin lid.

I leaned forward. Started to push up.

Cara and I both pushed with all our strength.

The heavy wooden lid didn't budge at first.

But then I heard a creaking sound as it started to lift.

Slowly, slowly, it raised up in our hands.

Leaning over the open coffin, we pushed it,

pushed it, until it stood straight up and came to a rest.

We let go of the lid.

I shut my eyes. I didn't really want to look inside.

But I had to.

I squinted down into the open coffin.

Too dark. I couldn't see a thing.

Good, I told myself. I let out a sigh of relief.

But then Cara bent down and picked up the flashlights from the floor. She slipped mine into my hand.

We aimed our lights into the coffin and stared inside.

The coffin was lined in purple velvet. The velvet glowed under the light from our flashlights. We swept our flashlights up and down the inside of the coffin.

"It — it's *empty*!" Cara stammered.

"No, it isn't," I replied.

My light locked on an object at the foot of the coffin. A spot of blue against the purple velvet.

As I moved closer, it came into focus.

A bottle. A blue glass bottle.

"Weird!" Cara exclaimed. Now she saw it, too.

"Yes. Totally weird," I agreed.

We both moved to the foot of the coffin to see it better. I pressed against the side of the coffin as I leaned close to the bottle. My hands felt frozen now.

Cara reached past me and picked up the bottle. She held it in the white beam of light from my flashlight, and we both studied it carefully.

The bottle was round and dark blue. It fit easily in Cara's hand. The glass was smooth. The bottle was closed by a blue glass stopper.

Cara shook it. "It's empty," she said softly.

"An empty bottle inside a coffin? Definitely weird!" I cried. "Who could have left it here?"

"Hey — there's a label." Cara pointed to a tiny square of paper glued to the glass. "Can you read it?" she asked. She raised the blue bottle to my face.

The tiny label had faded, old-fashioned-looking letters on it. I squinted hard.

The words had been rubbed until they were little more than smudges.

I held my light steady and finally managed to make out the words: "*VAMPIRE BREATH.*"

"Huh?" Cara's mouth opened in shock. "Did you say *Vampire Breath*?"

I nodded. "That's what it says."

"But what could that be?" she asked. "What is *Vampire Breath*?"

"Beats me," I replied, staring into the bottle. "I've never seen it advertised on TV!"

Cara didn't laugh at my joke.

She turned the bottle in her hands. She was looking for more information. But the label had only two words printed on it: "*VAMPIRE BREATH.*"

I turned my light back into the coffin to see if

we had missed anything inside it. I swept the light back and forth. Then I leaned over the side and rubbed my hand over the purple velvet. It felt smooth and soft.

When I looked back at Cara, she had tucked her flashlight under her arm. And she was twisting the glass stopper on top of the bottle.

"Hey — what are you doing?" I cried.

"Opening it," she replied. "But the top is stuck and I can't seem to —"

"No — !" I shouted. "Stop!"

Her dark eyes flashed. She locked them on mine. "Scared, Freddy?"

"Yes. I mean — no!" I stammered. "I — uh — I agree with you, Cara. We should wait for my parents to get home. We should show this to them. We can't just go around opening coffins and taking out bottles and —"

I gasped as she tugged at the stopper.

I wasn't afraid or anything. I just didn't want to do anything stupid.

"Give me that!" I shouted. I grabbed for the bottle.

"No way!" She swung around to keep me from getting it.

And the bottle fell out of her hand.

We both watched it hit the floor.

It landed on its side. Bounced once. Didn't break.

But the glass top popped off.

Cara and I both stared down at the bottle. Not breathing.

Waiting.

Wondering what would happen.

7

Sssssssssssssss.

It took me a few seconds to figure out what was making that hissing sound. Then I saw a smoky green mist shooting up from the bottle.

The thick mist rose up like a geyser, chilly and wet. I felt it float against my face.

"Ohhhh." I groaned when its sour smell reached my nose.

I staggered back, choking. I started to gag.

I thrashed both hands wildly, trying to brush the mist away.

"Yuck!" Cara cried, making a sick face. She pressed her fingers over her nose. "It *stinks*!"

The sickening fog swept around us. In seconds, the mist billowed all over the room.

"I — I can't breathe!" I gasped.

I couldn't see, either. The fog blocked the light from our flashlights!

"Ohhh," Cara groaned. "It smells so *bad*!"

My eyes burned. I could taste the sour fog on my

tongue. I felt sick. My stomach gurgled. My throat tightened.

I've got to plug up the bottle, I decided. If I close the bottle, this disgusting mist will stop spurting up.

I dropped to my knees and my flashlight clattered to the floor. I felt blindly along the floor till I found the bottle. Then I swept my other hand in a circle till my fingers curled around the stopper.

Struggling not to gag, I shoved the stopper into the top of the bottle.

I jumped to my feet and held the bottle up so that Cara could see that I closed it.

She didn't see me. She had both hands over her face. Her shoulders were heaving up and down.

As I set the bottle down, I started to gag. I swallowed hard. Again. Again. I couldn't get the disgusting taste from my mouth.

The sour fog swirled around us for a few seconds more. Then it lowered itself to the floor, fading away.

"Cara — ?" I finally choked out. "Cara — are you okay?"

She slowly lowered her hands from her face. She blinked several times, then turned to me. "Yuck," she murmured. "It was so gross! Why did you grab the bottle like that? That was all your fault."

"Huh?" I gasped. "My fault? My fault?"

She nodded. “Yes. If you hadn’t grabbed at the bottle, I never would have dropped it. And —”

“But *you’re* the one who wanted to open it!” I shrieked. “Remember? You were pulling off the top!”

“Oh.” She remembered.

She brushed at her sweater and jeans with both hands. She tried to wipe the awful smell away. “Freddy, let’s get out of here,” she demanded.

“Yeah. Let’s go.” For once we agreed on something.

I followed her to the door. Halfway across the room, I turned back.

Gazed at the coffin.

And gasped.

“Cara — look!” I whispered.

Someone was lying in the coffin.

8

Cara screamed. She grabbed my arm and squeezed it so hard, I cried out.

We huddled together in the doorway, staring back into the dark room.

Staring at the pale form in the coffin.

"Are you scared?" Cara whispered.

"Who — me?" I choked out.

I had to show her I wasn't scared. I took a step toward the coffin. Then another. She stayed close by my side. The beams of light from our flashlights darted shakily ahead of us.

My heart started to pound. My mouth suddenly felt dry. It was impossible to hold the flashlight steady.

"It's an old man," I whispered.

"But how did he get there?" Cara whispered back. "He wasn't there a second ago." She squeezed my arm again.

But I didn't really feel the pain. I was too excited, too amazed, too *confused* to feel anything.

How *did* he get there?

Who *was* he?

"Is he dead?" Cara asked.

I didn't answer. I crept up to the coffin and shone my light in.

The man was old and completely bald. His skin stretched tight against his skull, smooth as a lightbulb.

His eyes were shut. His lips were as pale as his skin, drawn tightly together.

He had tiny, white hands. Thin as bones. They were crossed over his chest.

He was dressed in a black tuxedo. Very old-fashioned-looking. The stiff collar of his white shirt pressed up against his pale cheeks. His shiny black shoes were buttoned instead of laced.

"Is he dead?" Cara repeated.

"I guess so," I choked out. I had never seen a dead person before.

Again, I felt Cara's hand on my arm. "Let's go," she whispered. "Let's get *out* of here!"

"Okay."

I wanted to leave. I wanted to get away from there as fast as I could.

But something held me there. Something froze me in place, staring at the pale, old face. At the old man lying so still, so silent in the purple coffin.

And as I stared, the old man opened his eyes.

Blinked.

And started to sit up.

9

I gasped and stumbled backward. If I hadn't hit the wall, I think I would have fallen over.

The flashlight fell from my hand. It clattered loudly to the floor.

The sound made the old man turn in our direction.

In the trembling beam from Cara's flashlight, he blinked several times. Then his tiny pale hands rubbed his eyes, as if rubbing the sleep from them.

He groaned softly. And tried to focus on us, squinting and rubbing his eyes.

My heart pounded so hard I thought it was about to explode through my shirt. My temples throbbed, and I let out sharp, wheezing breaths.

"I — I —" Cara stammered. I could see her whole body shaking as she stood in front of me, training the light on the old man in the coffin.

"Where am I?" the old man croaked. He shook

his head. He appeared dazed. "Where am I? What am I doing here?" He squinted in the flashlight beam.

His pale, bald head glowed in the light. Even his eyes were pale, sort of silvery.

He licked his white lips. His mouth made a dry, smacking sound.

"I'm so thirsty," he moaned in a hoarse whisper. "I'm so terribly — thirsty."

He sat up slowly, with a loud groan. As he pulled himself up, I saw that he wore a cape, a silky, purple cape that matched the purple of the coffin.

He licked his pale lips again. "So thirsty . . ."

And then he saw Cara and me.

He blinked again. And squinted at us. "Where am I?" he asked, staring hard at me with those eerie, silver eyes. "What room is this?"

"It's my house," I replied. But the words tumbled out in a weak whisper.

"So thirsty . . ." he murmured again. Groaning and muttering to himself, he lifted one leg over the coffin, then the other.

He slid out onto the floor. He didn't make a sound when he landed. He seemed so light, as if he didn't weigh anything at all.

A chill of fear froze the back of my neck. I tried to back up. But I was already pressed against the wall.

I glanced to the open doorway. It seemed a hundred miles away.

The old man licked his dry lips. Still squinting hard, he took a step toward Cara and me. He smoothed his cape with both hands as he walked.

"Who — are — you?" Cara managed to choke out.

"How did you get here?" I cried, finding my voice. "What are you doing in my basement? How did you get in that coffin?" The questions burst out of me. "Who are you?"

He stopped and scratched his bald head. For a moment, he appeared to be struggling to remember who he was.

Then he replied, "I am Count Nightwing." He nodded, as if reminding himself. "Yes. I am Count Nightwing."

Cara and I both uttered gasps. Then we started talking at the same time.

"How did you get here?"

"What do you want?"

"Are you — are you — a vampire?"

He covered his ears with his hands. He shut his eyes. "The noise . . ." he complained. "Please, speak softly. I've been asleep for so long."

"Are you a vampire?" I asked softly.

"Yes. A vampire. Count Nightwing." He nodded. And opened his eyes. He gazed at Cara, then at me, as if seeing us for the first time.

"Yessss," he hissed. He raised his arms and began to move toward us.

"And I'm so thirsty. So very thirsty. I've been asleep for so long. And now I'm thirsty. And I must drink now."

10

The count raised his arms and gripped the purple cape. The cape spread out behind him like wings, and he rose up into the air.

"So thirsty . . ." he murmured, licking his dry lips. "So thirsty." His silvery eyes locked onto Cara, as if trying to hypnotize her and hold her in place.

I was never so frightened in all my life. I admit it.

I don't scare easily. And neither does Cara.

We've watched a hundred vampire movies on TV. We laugh at them. We think the idea of a guy with fangs who flies around drinking human blood is funny.

We have never been the least bit scared.

But that was movies. This was *real life*!

We had just watched this guy — who called himself Count Nightwing — rise up from a coffin. A coffin practically in my basement!

And now, he had his arms spread out and he

was floating across the room toward us. Muttering about how thirsty he was. Narrowing his weird, frightening eyes at Cara's throat!

So, yes — I admit I was scared. But not too scared to move.

"Hey — !" I gasped and grabbed Cara's arm. "Come on!" I cried. "Let's *go*!"

She didn't budge.

"Cara — come *on*!" I screamed, tugging her.

She stared up at the pale face of the vampire.

She didn't move. She didn't blink.

I grabbed her arm with both hands. I tried to drag her away. But she stood rooted to the floor. As frozen as a statue.

"So thirsty . . ." the old man croaked. "I must drink now!"

"Cara — snap out of it!" I cried. "Snap out of it! Please!"

I pulled with all my strength — and dragged her to the door.

As we reached the tunnel, Cara blinked and shook her head. Letting out a startled cry, she tugged her arm free and started to run.

We both burst out of the little room and ran through the curving tunnel. Our shoes clapped loudly on the hard stone floor. The noise echoed off the walls. It sounded as if a *thousand* kids were running from the vampire!

My legs felt rubbery and weak. But I forced myself to run.

We ran through the dark tunnel, following the curve of the stone walls. Cara leaned forward, her arms stretched in front of her as she ran.

She gripped the flashlight tightly in one hand. The light bounced all over. But we didn't need it. We knew where we were running.

Cara is a very fast runner — faster than me. As we turned again, her long legs were pumping hard, and she was pretty far ahead of me.

I glanced back.

Was the vampire following us?

Yes.

He was close behind, floating near the ceiling, his cape flapping behind him.

"Cara — wait up!" I called breathlessly.

A yellow rectangle of light came into view up ahead.

The door! The door to my basement!

If we can just get to the door, I thought.

If we can get to my basement, we can slam the door behind us. And trap Count Nightwing in the tunnel.

If we can get to the basement, we'll be safe.

Mom and Dad must be home by now, I decided. *Please be home! Please!*

Up ahead, the rectangle of light from the open doorway grew larger.

Cara was running hard, uttering a low gasp with each step. I was several feet behind her now. Running as fast as I could. Struggling to catch up.

I didn't turn around. But I could hear the flap of the vampire's cape close behind me.

Cara had nearly reached the door.

Go, Cara, go! I thought. My chest felt about to burst. But I ran harder, desperate to catch up. To reach the door. To leap into the basement to safety.

"Ohhhh!" I cried out as I saw the rectangle of light start to grow smaller. "The door — it's closing!" I shrieked.

"Nooooooo!" Cara and I both wailed.

The door slammed shut with a crash.

Cara couldn't stop in time. She hit the door. And bounced off, stunned.

I grabbed her by the shoulders to steady her. "Are you okay?"

She didn't answer. Her eyes went to the closed door. She grabbed for the doorknob.

"Freddy —" she murmured. "Look!"

No doorknob! There *was* no knob on this side of the door.

With a frantic cry, I lowered my shoulder to the wooden door — and heaved my body against it. Again. Again.

Nothing happened.

My shoulder throbbed with pain. But the door didn't budge.

"Help!" I shouted. "Somebody — help! Let us out!"

Too late.

Count Nightwing had us trapped.

He landed silently, his cape lowering around him. A thin smile spread over his pale face. His silvery eyes opened wide with excitement. His tongue darted back and forth over his caked, dry lips.

"Run past him," Cara whispered in my ear. "Run back into the tunnel. Maybe we can keep him chasing after us and wear him out."

But the vampire raised his cape to block our way.

Could he read our minds?

Holding his cape high, he stepped up to Cara. "So thirsty . . ." he murmured. "So thirsty."

Then he lowered his face to Cara's throat.

11

"Let her go! Let her go!" I screamed.

I grasped at his waist, desperate to pull him away.

But I grabbed only cape.

"Let her go! Stop!" I pleaded, tugging on the cape.

I couldn't see Cara at all. I could see only the vampire's cape and shoulders as he lowered his head to drink her blood.

"Please — !" I begged. "I'll get you something *else* to drink! Please — let Cara go!"

To my surprise, Count Nightwing raised his head. He stood up straight and took a step back from Cara.

Cara raised her hand to her throat. She rubbed her neck. Her eyes were wide with fear, and her chin was quivering.

"Something is wrong," Count Nightwing said, shaking his head. He frowned. "Something is terribly wrong."

I turned to Cara. "Did he bite you?" I choked out.

Cara rubbed her neck. "No," she whispered.

"Something is wrong," the vampire repeated softly. He raised a hand to his mouth.

I watched him open his mouth and stick a finger inside. He shut his eyes and poked around in there.

"My fangs!" he cried finally. His strange eyes bulged and his mouth dropped open. "My fangs! They're gone!"

He turned away and started examining his mouth again.

I saw my chance. I pounded on the door to the basement with both fists. "Mom! Dad! Can you hear me?" I shouted.

Count Nightwing paid no attention to me. I heard him moan behind me. "My beautiful fangs!" he cried. "Gone. Gone. I'll *starve* to death without my fangs!"

He opened his mouth wide, showing Cara and me. He had no fangs. No teeth at all. Only gums.

"We're safe!" I whispered to Cara.

He's too old and weak to hurt us, I told myself. Without his fangs, the old vampire can't harm us.

"We're safe! We're safe!" I cried.

How wrong could a person be?

12

The old vampire poked a finger around in his mouth, shaking his head sadly the whole while. Finally, he sighed and dropped his hands to his sides.

"Doomed," he whispered. "Doomed. Unless . . ."

"Sorry we can't help you," I said. "Now, will you open the door and let me back in my house?"

Count Nightwing rubbed his chin. He shut his eyes, thinking hard.

"Yes. Let us out!" Cara insisted. "We can't help you. So —"

The old vampire's eyes shot open. "But you *can* help me!" he declared. "You *will* help me!"

I took a deep breath. "No. We *won't*," I told him. "Let us go — now."

He floated up over us. He moved his gaze from Cara to me. His silvery eyes suddenly appeared cold, icy. "You will help me," he said softly. "Both of you. If you ever hope to return to your homes again."

I shivered. The tunnel suddenly felt so cold, as if a freezing wind was blowing through it.

I glanced at the door. So close, I thought. We're so close to being safe and sound in my house.

On the other side of the door we would be out of danger. But we can't get there. We can't. We could be a thousand miles away.

I turned back to the icy stare of the old vampire.

He's evil, I realized. Even without his fangs, he is evil.

"Wh-what do we have to do?" Cara stammered.

"Yes. What can we do?" I repeated.

He lowered himself to the floor. His expression softened.

"The bottle of *Vampire Breath*," he said. "Did you see it?"

"Yes," I replied. "We found it. In your coffin."

"Do you have it?" he demanded eagerly. He reached out a hand. "Do you have it? Give it to me."

"No," Cara and I answered together.

"We didn't take it," I told him. "I think I left it on the floor."

"We — we dropped it," Cara stammered.

The old vampire gasped. "You *what*? Did you break it? Did you spill the *Vampire Breath*?"

"It — it poured out," I replied. "The room filled with smoke. We put the cap back on. But —"

"We must find it!" Count Nightwing declared. "I must have that bottle. If there is a little bit of *Vampire Breath* left in the bottle, it will take me back to my time."

"Your time?" I asked.

He squinted at me. "Your clothing. Your hair. You two are not of my time," he said. "What year is this?"

I told him.

His mouth dropped open. A startled squeak escaped his throat. "I have been asleep for over a hundred years!" he exclaimed. "I must find the *Vampire Breath*. It will take me back in time. Back to when I had my fangs."

I stared hard at him, trying to understand what he was telling us. "Does that mean you will go away?" I asked. "If there is *Vampire Breath* left in the bottle, you will go back a hundred years?"

The old vampire nodded. "Yessss," he hissed. "I will go back to my time." But then his eyes turned cold again. "*If* there is any of the precious *Vampire Breath* left," he said bitterly. "If you didn't spill it all."

"There's *got* to be some left!" I cried.

Cara and I followed Count Nightwing back through the tunnel. He floated silently ahead of us, his cape fluttering behind him. "So thirsty . . ." he kept muttering. "So terribly thirsty."

"I can't believe we're going back into that room," I whispered to Cara as we jogged over the smooth stone floor. "I can't believe we're going to help a vampire!"

"We have no choice," she replied. "We want to get rid of him — don't we?"

My shoes splashed through a puddle on the floor. I felt cold water on my ankles. The tunnel curved, and we followed it. Into the small, square room.

Count Nightwing stepped up to his coffin, then turned back to us. "Where is the bottle?" he demanded.

I picked up my flashlight from the floor. I clicked it. Once. Twice. No light. It must have broken when I dropped it. I set it back down on the floor.

"The bottle," the old vampire repeated. "I must have it."

"I think Freddy dropped it into the coffin," Cara told him. She stepped to the center of the room and flashed her light up and down the purple velvet of the coffin.

"No. It is not there," Count Nightwing said impatiently. "Where is it? You must find it. You have no idea how thirsty I am. It's been at least one hundred years!"

He's a good sleeper! I thought.

"It must be somewhere on the floor," Cara told him.

"Well, find it! *Find* it!" the vampire shrieked.

Cara and I began to search the floor. I walked beside her since she had the only light.

She swept the flashlight up and down the bare floors. No sign of the blue bottle.

"Where is it?" I whispered. "Where?"

"It shouldn't be so hard to find in an empty room!" Cara declared.

"Do you think maybe it rolled out into the tunnel?" I suggested.

Cara bit her bottom lip. "I don't think so." She raised her eyes from the floor and gazed at me. "We didn't break it — did we?"

"No. When I put the cap back on it, I set it down somewhere," I replied.

I glanced up to see the vampire glaring at us angrily. "I'm losing my patience," he warned. He licked his dry lips. His icy eyes moved from me to Cara.

"There it is!" Cara cried. Her beam of light froze at the base of the coffin. The blue bottle lay there on its side.

I charged across the room, bent quickly, and picked up the *Vampire Breath*.

Count Nightwing's eyes flashed in excitement. A pale smile spread over his face. "Open it — now!" he ordered. "Open it, and I will be gone. Back to my time. Back to my beautiful castle. Good-bye, children. Good-bye. Open it! Quickly!"

My hands trembled. I gripped the blue bottle

tightly in my left hand. I lowered my right hand to the glass stopper on top of the bottle.

I grabbed the stopper — and pulled it off the bottle.

And waited.

And waited.

Nothing happened.

13

And then I heard a *whoosh*.

I nearly dropped the bottle as a green mist sprayed up through the top.

"Yessss!" I cried happily. The bottle wasn't empty!

The sickening odor made me gasp, then hold my breath. But I didn't care about the smell.

I watched the fog thicken, thicken until I couldn't see the coffin in the middle of the room. Couldn't see Cara. Couldn't see the old vampire.

The dark mist billowed and swirled.

I wanted to cheer and jump up and down. Because I knew that Count Nightwing would disappear into the fog. And we would be safe. We would never see him again.

"Cara — are you okay?" I called. My voice sounded hollow, muffled by the swirling fog.

"It *stinks*!" she choked out.

"Hold your breath," I told her. "The last time, it faded away in a few seconds."

"It's soooo disgusting!" she wailed.

Cara was standing close beside me. But I couldn't see her in the waves of mist.

So damp and cold. I suddenly felt as if I were standing under water. Standing under the ocean as wave after wave rolled over me.

I held my breath as long as I could. When my chest started to burn, I let it out in a long *whoosh.*

I shut my eyes and prayed. Prayed for the fog to fade, for the mist to lower to the floor and disappear, as it had before.

Please, please — I thought. Don't let Cara and me drown in this disgusting mist.

A few seconds later, I opened my eyes.

Darkness all around.

I blinked several times. A square of pale yellow light glowed in the distance.

Moonlight pouring in through a window.

Window? There *is* no window in this room! I told myself.

I turned and saw Cara. She was swallowing hard, her eyes wide, glancing nervously around the room. "He — he's gone," she murmured. "Freddy — the vampire is gone."

I squinted into the dim light. "But where *are* we?" I whispered. I pointed to the open window far away, at the other end of the room. "There was no window before."

Cara chewed her bottom lip. "We're not in the

same room," she said softly. "This room is so big and —" She stopped.

"Coffins!" I cried.

As my eyes adjusted to the light, the low, solid shapes formed out of the shadows. And I realized I was staring at two long, straight rows of coffins.

"Where *are* we?" Cara cried, unable to hide the fear in her voice. "It must be some sort of graveyard or something!"

"But we're indoors," I said. "We're not in a graveyard. We're in a room. A very long room."

I gazed up to the high ceilings. Two glass chandeliers hung down, their crystals gleaming dully in the pale moonlight.

The dark walls were covered with huge paintings. Even in the dim light, I could see that they were portraits, portraits of stern-faced men and women in formal, old-fashioned, black clothes.

I turned back to the rows of coffins — and silently started to count them. "There must be two dozen coffins in this room!" I whispered to Cara.

"All lined up so perfectly in two straight rows," she added. "Freddy, do you think — ?"

"He took us with him," I murmured.

"Huh?" Cara chewed her lip.

"Count Nightwing. He took us with him," I repeated. "He was supposed to go back to his castle — by himself. He said he would go and never see us again. But he took us with him, Cara. I'm sure he did."

Cara stared straight ahead at the rows of coffins. "But he can't *do* that!" she cried. "He can't!"

I started to reply. But a sound made me stop.

A creaking sound.

I felt a chill sweep down my back as I heard another creaking, closer this time.

Cara grabbed my arm. She heard it too. "Freddy — look!" she whispered.

I squinted into the dim light. "The coffins — !" I whispered.

They were all creaking open.

14

The coffin lids raised up slowly. I could see pale hands pushing them up from inside. Creaking, the lids swung open, then stopped.

Cara and I huddled together, unable to move. Unable to take our eyes off the terrifying sight.

I heard low moans and groans as the vampires sat up. Bony hands gripped the sides of the coffins. I heard coughing. Dry throats being cleared.

The vampires pulled themselves up slowly. Their faces were yellow in the moonlight. Their eyes gleamed dully, a pale silver.

"Ohhhhhhh." Groans echoed off the high walls. Bones creaked and cracked.

They looked so old. Older than the oldest people you see on the street. Their skin appeared so thin and was wrapped so tight, you could see the bones underneath.

Living skeletons, I thought. Their ancient bones snapped as they moved.

"Ohhhhhh." They pulled themselves up. Legs, thin as spider legs, reached over the coffin sides.

Cara and I finally moved. We backed into the deep shadows against the wall.

I heard more coughing. Near the window, a white-haired vampire leaned over the edge of his coffin, making ugly choking sounds.

"So thirsty . . ." I heard one of them whisper.

"So thirsty . . . so thirsty . . ." others repeated.

They lowered themselves from their coffins, stretching and groaning.

"So thirsty . . . so thirsty . . ." they chanted. Their voices were dry and raspy, as if their throats were sore, as if their voices were only air.

They were all dressed in black. Formal black suits. White shirt collars stiff and high over their chins. Some of them wore long, shiny capes. They adjusted their capes with bony, white fingers, sweeping them back over bent, skinny shoulders.

"So thirsty . . . so thirsty . . ." Their silver eyes glowed brighter as they began to wake up.

And then, standing in the aisle between the two rows of coffins, they began to flap their bony arms. Slowly at first. Their arms creaked as they pulled them up, then down.

The silver eyes glowed in the pale, old faces.

Up, then down. Up, then down. They flapped their arms faster, groaning and grunting. The sound echoed off the walls and the high ceiling.

Flapping faster now. Flapping. Flapping.

And as Cara and I gaped in amazement, the sickly, groaning old men began to shrink. The flapping arms became the flutter of black wings. The red eyes glowed from rodent-like faces.

In seconds, they shrank and transformed. They all became fluttering, black bats.

And turned their red eyes to Cara and me.

15

Did they see us?

Could they see us in the deep darkness, our backs pressed against the stone wall?

The bats fluttered up over the open coffins. Their flapping wings glistened, silvery in the moonlight.

I heard a rattling, like the warning sound of a snake. But the rattling quickly became a *hiss*.

The bats opened their mouths, revealing pointed yellow fangs — and hissed. What a sound! A shrill, angry whistle that rose higher, higher, until it drowned out the patter of their fluttering wings.

A *hiss* of attack.

They were awake and ready now. Ready to swoop at me, to knock me to the floor, to dig those pointed fangs deep into my skin. And drink . . . drink . . .

"Freddy — !" Cara cried. She raised her hands in front of her to shield her face. "Freddy — !"

The shrill hissing surrounded me. Seemed to be coming from *inside* my head. I covered my ears, trying to shut it out.

Covered my ears. Watched their red, glowing eyes — and waited for the attack.

But to my shock, the hissing bats didn't swoop toward us.

They fluttered up, up. Turned. And flapped in a line out the open window at the other end of the room.

My mouth hung open. I realized I had stopped breathing.

I watched them fade into the moonlight, shiny wings fluttering rapidly, the shrill hissing fading with them.

Then I took a deep breath and slowly let it out. "Cara," I whispered. "We're okay. They didn't see us back here."

She nodded but didn't reply. A thick strand of her black hair had become matted to her forehead. She brushed it back with a trembling hand.

"Wow," she murmured, shaking her head. "Wow."

"We're okay," I repeated. My eyes checked out the long room. The open coffins stretched to the window. Their dark wood gleamed in the moonlight. Their long shadows crept along the floor.

"We're okay now," I repeated to Cara. "We're all alone."

Footsteps behind us made us both cry out.

I heard a throat being cleared.

I spun around so hard, I nearly toppled over.

Count Nightwing strode into the room carrying a flaming torch. The torchlight flickered over his smooth face. His silvery eyes were wide with surprise.

"What are you two doing here?" he demanded.

I opened my mouth to reply. But a sputtering, choking sound was all I could force out.

"You do not belong here," the old vampire boomed. He waved the fiery torch in front of him. It left a trail of orange light as he swung it. "You have no right to be here. This is my time. And this is my castle."

He floated off the floor. His eyes suddenly glowed as brightly as the torch flame. "You do not belong here!" he repeated menacingly.

"But — but —" I stammered, frightened and angry and confused — all at the same time.

"But you brought us here!" Cara protested angrily. She waved her finger at him, accusing him. "We didn't follow you!"

"She's right!" I finally found my voice. "You promised us you would go away and leave us alone. But you brought us back to your castle with you."

Still floating a few feet above the floor, Count Nightwing held the torch in one hand and rubbed his frail-looking chin with the other. "Hmmmmmm," he murmured. His eyes glowed at us. "Hmmmmm."

"You have to send us home," Cara told him, pressing her hands against her waist.

"Yes!" I agreed. "Send us home — now."

Count Nightwing lowered himself silently to the floor. In the flickering torchlight, he suddenly looked weary. The light in his eyes dulled. He sighed.

"Just send us home," Cara insisted. "We won't tell anyone we saw you. We'll forget this whole thing happened."

The old vampire brushed back his cape. He shook his head. "I can't send you home," he whispered.

"Why not?" I demanded.

He sighed again. "I don't know how."

"Huh?" Cara and I both gasped.

"I don't know how to send you home," Count Nightwing repeated. "I'm a vampire — not a magician."

"But — but — but —" I started sputtering again. My whole body shook in total panic.

"Then what are we going to do?" Cara demanded shrilly.

The old vampire shrugged again. "It's really no problem," he replied softly. "No problem at all. As soon as I find my fangs, I'll drink your blood. And I'll turn you both into vampires."

16

"But we want to go home!" I screamed.

"We don't *want* to be vampires!" Cara wailed. "This isn't fair! We helped you. Now you have to help *us*!"

The old vampire didn't hear us. In the flickering orange light from the torch, I saw his eyes go all dreamy. His whole body appeared to flicker in and out with the light.

"The *Vampire Breath*," he whispered. "I need it — now."

"Send us home — now!" Cara ordered him. "I mean it. Send us home!"

I balled my hands into fists. I felt so angry!

I mean, we helped him return to his castle. And how was he going to pay us back?

By biting our necks and turning us into vampires. By keeping us here forever.

I tried to imagine what it would be like living here in this castle. Sleeping all day in a coffin.

Rising up at night and turning into a bat. Flying out night after night in search of necks to bite.

Forever.

Just thinking about it made me shake with horror.

I'll never complain about having to baby-sit for Tyler Brown again, I decided.

And then the horrifying thought made my heart skip: I may never see Tyler Brown again.

Or Mom and Dad. Or any of my friends.

"You've *got* to send us home!" I cried to Count Nightwing. "You've *got* to!"

He was pacing back and forth in front of us now, the torchlight dipping and darting. He didn't pay any attention to us. I don't think he even remembered that Cara and I were in the room.

"*Vampire Breath*," he repeated. "I must find the *Vampire Breath*."

Where *is* the bottle of *Vampire Breath*? I wondered. I was holding it in my hand when we opened it back in the little room.

My eyes searched the floor. No sign of the little blue bottle.

It must have disappeared when we traveled back in time, I realized.

"Why do you need it?" Cara asked.

The old vampire narrowed his eyes at her. "When he is awake, a vampire needs *Vampire*

Breath every day," he said softly. "We cannot live by blood alone."

Cara and I both stared at him, waiting for him to continue. "We all live together, here in my castle," he explained in his hoarse, whispery voice. "We live here so we can be close to our supply of *Vampire Breath*. We each have our own bottles. We guard them closely."

He sighed. "But now I remember — the supply was running low. I was down to my last bottle. I must find it. I *must*!"

"But what does it do for you?" I demanded.

"Everything!" Count Nightwing shouted. "*Vampire Breath* does everything for a vampire! It allows us to travel in time. It can make us invisible and reappear again. It keeps our skin smooth and clear. It gives us energy. It helps us sleep. It keeps our bones from drying to powder. It freshens our breath!"

"Wow," I murmured, shaking my head.

"But how will it help you find your fangs?" Cara demanded.

"*Vampire Breath* restores the memory," the old vampire told her. "When you live for hundreds of years, it's hard to remember things. The *Vampire Breath* will help me remember where I put my fangs."

He spun around. His eyes locked on me. "The bottle. Do you still have it?"

I could feel the power of his silvery eyes. I could feel them burning into me, searching my mind.

"N-no — !" I stammered. "I don't have it."

"But it won't do you any good!" Cara cried. "We emptied it, remember? We emptied the whole bottle to get you back here."

Count Nightwing shook his head impatiently. "That was in the future," he snapped. "That was over a hundred years in the future. This is 1880, remember? In 1880, the bottle is still full."

My head was spinning. I leaned against a coffin and tried to make sense of what he was saying.

The old vampire started to pace again, rubbing his chin thoughtfully. "I hid the bottle somewhere," he muttered. "I hid it so that the others couldn't find it and use it while I took my nap. But where? Where did I hide it? I must find it. I *must*."

He spun away from us, his long purple cape swirling behind him. The orange torchlight bounced ahead of him as he floated toward the doorway. "Where? Where?" he asked himself, shaking his head.

A few seconds later, he vanished.

Cara and I were left alone with the rows of coffins in the long room. Cara sighed unhappily. She motioned to the coffins. "I hope I get one near the window," she joked. "I like a lot of fresh air."

I was still leaning against the nearest coffin. I stood up and slapped the side angrily with my hand. "I don't believe this!" I cried.

"I'm only twelve," Cara moaned. "I'm not ready to die and then live forever!"

I swallowed hard. "You know what we have to do — don't you?" I said softly. "We have to find the *Vampire Breath* before Count Nightwing does. If he finds it first and gets his fangs back, we're doomed."

"I don't agree," Cara replied sharply. "I have a much better plan."

"A better plan? What is it?" I demanded.

17

Cara glanced to the doorway, then back to me. "We have to get out of here," she whispered.

"That's your plan?" I exclaimed. "That's it? That's a plan?"

She nodded and raised a finger to her lips. "Maybe if we run away from the castle, we can find help," she explained. "If we stay here, we're doomed no matter what we do. If we stay here, we're in his power."

"How is anyone going to help us?" I argued. "This is over a hundred years ago — remember? How will anyone outside the castle help us get back home to the future?"

"I don't know," Cara replied unhappily. "I only know that if we stay here in this creepy castle, we don't stand a chance."

I opened my mouth to argue some more. But I couldn't think of anything else to say.

Cara was probably right. Our only chance was to escape.

"Come on," she whispered. She grabbed my hand and started to pull me along the rows of coffins.

I held back. "Where are we going?"

She pointed. "To the window. Let's see if we can climb out."

The room was as long as our school gym. We walked quickly between the two rows of open coffins. I couldn't take my eyes off the old wooden coffins.

Vampires sleep inside them.

Those were the words that floated through my mind as we hurried past them.

Cara and I may soon sleep in them, too.

I shivered. And stopped. "Cara, look." I pointed to the window up ahead. "This is a waste of time."

She sighed. She saw what I meant. The big window was set very high up in the wall. It stood way over our heads.

We couldn't reach it even if we had a ladder.

"The only way to get through that window is to fly," I said softly.

Cara frowned and stared up at the window. "I hope you and I don't spend the rest of our lives flapping our bat wings and flying in and out of that window," she said.

"There's *got* to be a way out of this castle," I told her, forcing myself to sound cheerful. "Come on. Let's find the front door."

"Freddy — no." Cara pulled me back. "We

can't just go running down the halls. Count Nightwing will see us."

"We'll be careful," I said. "Come on, Cara. We'll find a way out."

We turned and jogged side by side past the empty coffins. Through the door. And into a long, dimly lit hallway.

The hall appeared to stretch for miles. Dark wood doors lined both sides. The doors were all closed. Above each door, a gas lamp provided a soft glow of yellow light.

My shoes sank into the thick, blue carpet. The air smelled sour. I glanced back at the coffin room. An ugly stone gargoyle leered down at me, perched above the door.

I turned away from its evil stare and gazed up and down the long hall. The rows of doors stretched in both directions. "Which way?" I whispered.

Cara shrugged. "It doesn't really matter. We just have to find a door or window that will take us outside."

We made our way silently over the thick carpet. The gas lamps cast a gloomy, dim light. Our shadows seemed to hide behind us as we walked.

Cara and I stopped at the first door we came to. I grabbed the brass knob and turned it. The heavy door creaked as it opened.

We peered into a large, square room filled with

furniture. The furniture was all covered with white sheets. Chairs rose up like ghosts beside a long, covered couch. In a corner beside a darkened fireplace, a grandfather clock stood guarding the room.

Cara pointed to the heavy black drapes that stretched over the far wall. "There must be a window behind there. Let's check it out."

We raced across the room. My shoes slipped on the floor. Glancing down, I saw nearly an inch of dust spread over the floor.

"I don't think this room has been used for a while," I said.

Cara didn't reply. She grabbed an end of the heavy drape and tugged. I reached to help her. The drape slid back. A dust-smeared window stood behind it.

"Great!" I cried.

"Not so great," Cara replied glumly.

I saw instantly what she meant. The window had thick black bars across it.

"Uggggh." With a disgusted groan, Cara shoved the drape back into place. We hurried back into the hall and tried the door across the hall. We stepped into a small room filled with luggage trunks. The trunks were stacked on top of each other up to the high ceiling.

No window in this room.

The next room had an enormous, old dark

wood desk in its center and shelves of ancient-looking books from floor to ceiling. Another heavy, black drape covered the window.

I eagerly pulled the drape back — to find another dust-covered window. And more thick, black bars. "Weird," I muttered.

"This castle is like a prison," Cara said in a shaky whisper. Her dark eyes glowed with fear. "But there has *got* to be a way out."

We crept back into the long hall. I stopped when I heard a soft fluttering sound.

Bat wings?

Were the vampires returning?

Cara heard it, too. "Hurry," she whispered.

We pushed open the next door and darted inside. I carefully closed the door behind us. Then I turned and saw that we had entered a big dining room.

The long table filled most of the room. It was bare except for a tall candelabra in its center. Stubs of white candles poked up in the candelabra. Wax had dripped in small puddles onto the tabletop. The puddles were buried in a gray layer of dust.

"No one has been in here in a long time," I muttered.

Cara was already at the window. She pulled back the drape to reveal another barred window.

"Aaaggggh!" She tore at her hair in frustration. "Every window! Every window has bars!"

she wailed. "And we can't keep walking through these halls. Someone will find us."

Staring at the long, dust-covered dining room table, I had an idea. "Vampires don't eat," I said.

"So what?" Cara cried. She slammed her fist against the heavy black drape.

"So they probably never go in the kitchen," I continued. "We'll be safe in the kitchen. And maybe there is a kitchen door. Maybe . . ."

Cara sighed. "Maybe. Maybe. Maybe." She shook her head glumly. "There are a thousand rooms in this creepy old castle. How will we even find the kitchen?"

I took her by the shoulders and guided her to the door. "Well, this is the dining room, right? Maybe the kitchen is close to the dining room."

"Maybe maybe maybe," she repeated bitterly.

I guided her into the hall, then led the way to the next door. We pushed it open and peeked inside.

No. Not the kitchen.

We quickly crept down the hall, trying door after door.

No kitchen. No kitchen.

We kept glancing back, watching for Count Nightwing, hoping we wouldn't bump into him.

We turned a corner. Found ourselves in a narrower, darker hallway. I tried the first door.

Yes!

An old-fashioned kitchen with a wide fireplace

hearth, a wood-burning stove, and blackened pots and pans hanging on the wall beside the hearth.

My eyes glanced quickly around the room. And landed at the broad kitchen window.

No black drape. *And no bars*!

"Yaaaay!" Cara cheered.

We both dove for the window. Could we open it?

We tried pushing it up from the bottom. But there were no handles, no place to grip the frame.

"Smash it!" Cara cried. "Smash the window open!"

I ran to the wall and pulled down a heavy metal skillet. I lugged it to the window. Pulled back my arm. Prepared to swing.

"Oh!" I cried out when I heard a cough.

Behind us. From the hallway.

"It's him!" I whispered. "It's Count Nightwing!"

"Smash the window!" Cara insisted.

"No. He'll hear us! He'll find us!" I whispered back.

I lowered the skillet to the floor. And turned back to study the window.

Another cough. Closer this time.

"Look," I whispered to Cara. "It pushes out, I think." I reached with both hands and pushed at the dust-smeared windowpane.

Leaned into it. Pushed with all my strength.

Slowly, slowly, the window slid out. With a groan, I pushed it open as far as it would go.

A gust of cool night air swept over me. I grabbed Cara's hand and started to give her a boost.

A noise behind us at the doorway made me jump. "Hurry — !" I whispered. "He's coming!"

My heart pounding, I pushed Cara up to the window. Then we both scrambled frantically out onto the ledge.

18

"Did he see us? Was he in the kitchen?" Cara whispered.

"I don't know," I told her. "I didn't see. But he was definitely in the hall."

"If he saw us . . ." Cara started. A gust of wind drowned out the rest of her words.

The night wind felt cool and refreshing on my skin. Heavy clouds floated over the full moon, plunging us into total darkness.

We were both on our knees, our backs to the kitchen. Huddled close beside Cara, I struggled to keep my balance on the narrow stone window ledge.

"Let's get going," I urged.

We both turned and faced the window. Then, gripping the stone ledge with both hands, we began lowering our legs down the wall, lowering ourselves to the ground.

Lower. Lower . . .

"Hey — !" I cried out when my feet didn't touch anything solid.

A shaft of moonlight broke through the clouds.

I looked down.

And opened my mouth in a hoarse scream.

My feet kicked the air. My hands gripped the ledge above me.

I stared down into empty space.

Far below I could see dark, jagged rocks glowing dully in the moonlight.

Far below!

Miles below!

"We — we're on top of a cliff!" Cara stammered. "The castle — it's built on a cliff!"

"Ohhhhh." I uttered a terrified moan.

The castle was built on top of a sheer rock cliff. And we were now dangling over the side. Dangling by our arms. Dangling . . .

My arms started to ache. I could feel my hands slipping, losing their grip on the stone window ledge above me.

"Cara — !" I gasped.

19

My hands scraped the dark stones of the wall.

I struggled to grab on to something — *anything*!

But I was falling too fast.

My feet kicked. I thrashed my arms. The wind rushed up at me as if trying to push me back up.

Was that *me* howling like that?

I was falling too fast to hear my own scream.

And then suddenly I stopped.

Stopped screaming. Stopped falling.

A black shadow swept around me. I felt something sharp dig into my shoulders. Hot breath grazed the back of my neck.

I heard a loud flapping sound. A fluttering heartbeat.

Gripped inside this shadow, I felt myself being pulled up.

I twisted my head back — and saw two glowing red eyes. The hot breath poured from its dark gaping mouth.

It's going to eat me! I realized.

I'm trapped inside this red-eyed shadow. Trapped in its talons as it carries me higher. Higher.

And then darkness surrounded me.

I landed somewhere. Landed hard on my feet with a loud *thud*.

The darkness lifted. I opened my eyes and saw Cara. Her mouth dropped open in amazement. "Freddy — !" she choked out. "Freddy — ?"

I spun toward the big open window to see the giant bat that had carried me back to the kitchen. Its wings flapped against the floor. The red eyes glowed angrily from its big, ugly face.

It saved our lives! I realized.

I collapsed to my knees. I grabbed the side of the stove to hold myself up.

I'm okay. I'm going to be okay, I told myself.

I raised my eyes to the enormous bat.

It started to shrink. It tucked itself inside its black wings. Wrapped the wings around its body.

The wings melted into a cape. A purple cape. And as the cape swept back, Count Nightwing appeared.

"You made a serious mistake, young man," he scolded sternly. His strange, silver eyes burned angrily into mine. "Did you think you could fly?" he demanded with a sneer. "You are not ready to fly — yet!"

"I — I — I —" I was still shaking too hard to speak.

"When I turn you into a vampire, you can fly every night," Count Nightwing snarled. He lowered his face close to mine, so close I could smell the decay of his pale skin. "Don't try to escape again," he growled. "It is a waste of time. And the next time . . . I won't catch you."

I swallowed hard. I held my breath, trying to force my heart to stop pounding so hard.

Count Nightwing turned away from me. Swirling the purple cape behind him, he floated past Cara, through the kitchen.

He stopped at the door and swung back to us. "Don't just stand there," he ordered. "Come help me find the *Vampire Breath*. I know it's somewhere in this wing of the castle."

He grabbed his pale throat. "I'm so thirsty . . . so thirsty." His silvery eyes locked on Cara, then on me. "I must remember where I hid my fangs. Hurry. Help find the *Vampire Breath*. It's somewhere nearby. I'm certain of it."

Cara and I had no choice. He stood at the doorway, waiting for us to follow him.

Holding on to the stove, I pulled myself to my feet. Then I followed Cara through the kitchen to the hall.

"Perhaps I hid the bottle in the royal guest room," Count Nightwing said, talking to himself. He pushed open a door and vanished inside the room.

Cara and I kept walking. The hallways appeared to stretch for *miles* ahead of us. Door after door after door. And this was only one wing of the old vampire's castle.

"Are you okay?" Cara asked, studying me as we walked. "You still look kind of shaky."

"I *am* kind of shaky," I confessed. "After all, I fell off a cliff!"

Cara shook her head. "It isn't going to be easy to escape."

"We can't escape," I replied. "The castle was built up here on top of the cliff to keep anyone from escaping."

She brushed a strand of black hair from her eyes. "We can't give up, Freddy. We have to keep trying. As soon as he finds his fangs, he's going to turn us into vampires."

"That's why my first plan is the best," I insisted. "We have to find the bottle of *Vampire Breath* before he does. Maybe we'll get lucky. Maybe we'll find it first."

"But what will we do with it once we have it?" Cara demanded.

"Mainly keep it from him!" I declared.

I pulled her into the next room. We both gasped when we saw the coffins.

Dozens of them. All lined up perfectly in four rows, the length of the room. All open.

"Another vampire bedroom!" Cara cried. She shivered. "It's so creepy, Freddy. Look how many there are!"

"The vampires are all out somewhere, swooping around, searching for blood to drink," I said. "But soon they'll be flying home. And when they see us . . ."

Cara gulped. "We'll be their dessert!"

"Uh . . . maybe we should search for the *Vampire Breath* in another room," I suggested. "Somewhere *away* from these coffins."

But then my eye fell on something. A coffin against the wall.

A *closed* coffin.

"Cara — look at that!" I whispered, pointing. "All the other coffins were left open. That's the only one with a closed lid. Do you think — ?"

Cara squinted at the closed coffin. "Weird," she murmured. "Very weird."

My brain whirred with crazy ideas. "Maybe it's an empty coffin," I suggested excitedly. "Maybe no one sleeps in that coffin. That would make it the perfect place. The perfect place to hide a bottle of *Vampire Breath*."

Cara held me back. "Or maybe a vampire is sleeping in the coffin," she warned. "If we open the coffin and wake him up . . ." Her voice trailed off.

"We have to look inside!" I exclaimed. "We have to take that chance."

We made our way to the coffin. I stared at the polished, dark wood of the lid. I cautiously ran a hand over the smooth wood.

Then, without saying a word, Cara grabbed one handle, and I grabbed the other. And slowly, slowly, we began to lift the coffin lid.

20

The lid was solid and heavy. Cara and I leaned into it and pushed. Finally, it dropped to the other side of the coffin.

I turned to the door to make sure Count Nightwing hadn't heard.

No sign of him.

I pulled myself up straight and peered into the open coffin. The inside was covered with dark green felt. It reminded me of the pool table in our basement.

I sighed. I wondered if I'd ever see my basement again.

"It's empty," Cara murmured sadly. "Just an empty coffin."

"We've got to keep searching," I said. I started to back away from the coffin when I saw the pocket.

A green pocket in the side of the coffin. Like the pockets on the sides of suitcases. It bulged out a little from the side.

"Whoa. Hold on a minute," I told Cara. She was already halfway to the door.

I reached into the pocket.

And pulled out a blue glass bottle.

"Cara — look!" I cried. I forgot that we didn't want Count Nightwing to hear us. "I found it! The *Vampire Breath*!"

A smile broke out over Cara's face. Her dark eyes flashed with excitement. "Excellent!" she exclaimed. "Excellent! Now we've got to hide it from Count Nightwing. Somewhere he'll *never* find it."

I held the bottle up close to my face and studied it. "Maybe we should open it and pour it all out," I said.

Cara rushed up beside me. She took the bottle from my hand. "When we opened it before, it took us back in time," she said excitedly. "Maybe if we opened it now . . ."

"It will take us forward in time!" I finished her thought for her. "Yes! Count Nightwing said it can be used for time travel. Maybe if we open it — and think real hard about where we want to go — it will take us home to my basement."

We both stared at the blue bottle.

Should we hide it and keep it away from the old vampire to stop him from getting back his fangs?

Or should we open it up and hope that the smelly mist would carry us home?

Cara gripped the bottle tightly in one hand.

She raised her other hand to the glass stopper on the top.

She started to pull it open — then stopped.

We stared at each other. We didn't speak.

"Go ahead. Do it," I whispered.

Cara nodded in agreement. She squeezed the stopper again and started to pull.

But she stopped once again. And gasped.

Out of the corner of my eye, I saw something move. I heard a soft footstep.

And I realized that we were no longer alone.

21

I spun around, expecting to find Count Nightwing.

"Oh!" I cried out when a girl stepped out of the shadows.

Her pale blue eyes were wide with shock. I think she was as surprised to see us as we were to see her!

As she stepped toward us, I saw that she had ringlets of blond curls that fell past her shoulders. She wore a gray jumper, very long and old-fashioned, with a white blouse underneath.

She's about our age, I realized. But definitely from a different time.

She stopped several coffins away. "Who are you?" she asked, eyeing us suspiciously. "What are you doing here?"

"We — we don't really know," I stammered.

"We know who we are. But we don't really know what we're doing here!" Cara corrected me.

"We got here by accident," I added.

The girl's confused expression didn't change. She tucked her hands into the pockets of her jumper.

"Who are *you*?" Cara demanded.

The girl didn't answer right away. Keeping her distance, she continued to study us with her pale blue eyes. "Gwendolyn," she said finally. "My name is Gwendolyn."

"Are you one of *them*?" The question popped out of my mouth.

Gwendolyn shuddered. "No," she answered quickly. Her mouth curled into an angry sneer. "No. I *hate* them!" she declared. "I hate them all!"

Cara shifted her weight tensely. I could see that she was really nervous. She handed the bottle of *Vampire Breath* to me. The bottle felt cold and damp from Cara's hands. I lowered it to my side, out of Gwendolyn's sight.

"Do you live here?" Cara asked Gwendolyn. "Are you related to Count Nightwing?"

Gwendolyn's sneer grew more bitter. "No," she choked out. Tears welled in her eyes. "I'm a prisoner here. I'm only twelve. But they treat me as a slave."

She let the tears run down her pale cheeks. "A slave," she repeated in a trembling voice. "Do you know what they force me to do? Clean and polish their coffins, night and day."

"Yuck," Cara murmured.

Gwendolyn sighed. She brushed her blond ringlets off her face and wiped away a tear. "Night and day. There are a dozen coffin rooms in this castle. All filled with row after row of coffins. And I must keep them smooth and shiny and clean for the vampires."

"What if you refuse?" I asked. "What if you tell Count Nightwing you won't do it anymore?"

Gwendolyn uttered a dry laugh. "Then he'll turn me into a vampire." She shuddered again. "I'd rather clean their coffins," she murmured bitterly.

"Can't you escape?" I asked.

Another dry laugh escaped her lips. "Escape? If I did, they would track me down. They would turn into bats and fly after me. And they would drink my blood until I was one of them."

I swallowed hard. I felt so bad for her. I didn't know what to say.

"We don't belong here," Cara told her, glancing to the door. "Count Nightwing brought us here by accident. Can you help us? Is there *any* way for us to escape?"

Gwendolyn lowered her gaze to the floor, thinking hard. "There may be a way," she said finally. "But we'll have to be very careful. If he catches us . . ."

"We'll be careful," I promised.

Gwendolyn glanced to the front of the room.

"Follow me," she whispered. "Hurry. It is almost dawn. If the vampires return and see you — it will be too late. They will pounce on you and drink your blood. You will never see daylight again."

She led us into the hall. Clinging to the wall, we stopped and looked in both directions.

No sign of Count Nightwing. But we knew he was nearby. Searching for the bottle of *Vampire Breath*. The bottle I held tightly in my hand.

"This way," Gwendolyn whispered.

We followed her through another door. It led to a narrow stairway. Gas lamps on the wall cast a dim glow, lighting the stairs as we made our way down.

We found ourselves in a long, twisting tunnel. Gwendolyn led us through it, walking rapidly, silently. The tunnel was so narrow, we had to walk single file. It twisted and curved, and took us down, deeper into the castle.

"Is there really a way out down here?" Cara asked Gwendolyn. Cara's voice echoed in the narrow tunnel.

Gwendolyn nodded. "Yes. Follow me. There is a secret exit through the castle cellar."

Our footsteps thudded on the hard tunnel floor. Up ahead of us, Gwendolyn's blond hair glowed like a torch leading the way.

The way to freedom. The way to safety.

I leaned close to Cara and whispered. "This is

great! We're getting out of here — and we're taking the *Vampire Breath* with us!"

Cara raised a finger to her lips. "We're not out yet," she reminded me.

The tunnel emptied into a huge, dark cellar. Gwendolyn pulled a flaming torch off the wall and carried it high in front of her to light our way.

"Follow me," she whispered. "Hurry."

The flickering torch cast a narrow path of light through the cellar. I couldn't see anything on either side of us. Total blackness.

Gwendolyn led us deeper into the darkness. It smelled damp and sour down here. Somewhere in the distance I heard water dripping.

Cara and I huddled close together, trying to stay in the light of the torch. I squeezed the bottle of *Vampire Breath* tightly in my hand.

Gwendolyn stopped so suddenly, we nearly walked into her.

She turned slowly. The torchlight revealed a smile on her face.

"Are we here?" Cara demanded. "Where is the door?"

"Yes. We're here," Gwendolyn replied in a whisper. "We're all alone here."

"Huh?" I cried. I didn't understand.

"I have you all to myself here," Gwendolyn continued. Her smile grew wider. Her eyes were half-shut. "We won't be interrupted by Count Nightwing or the others."

"But — where do we escape?" I demanded.

Gwendolyn didn't reply.

"Why have we stopped here?" Cara cried.

"I'm so thirssssty. . . ." Gwendolyn hissed. "So thirsssty . . ."

As she lowered the torch, I saw long, pointed fangs slide down her chin.

"I'm so thirsty. . . ." She sighed. "So terribly thirsty . . ."

She grabbed me by the shoulders. And I felt the scratch of her fangs against my throat.

22

"No — !" I screamed.

I grabbed her arms and shoved her off me.

"No! Get away! Get away from me!" I howled.

Her eyes flashed excitedly. Saliva dripped from her pointed fangs. "So thirsssssty . . ." she hissed.

"Get away! Get away!" I pleaded.

"You want to escape, don't you?" she teased. "This is the only way to escape!"

She tossed back her head and opened her mouth wide. Then she dove for me.

"No way!" I cried. I ducked away. Her long, curly hair slapped against my face. I staggered back. Caught my balance.

She prepared to attack again.

"Freddy — the *Vampire Breath*!" Cara cried. "Use the *Vampire Breath*! Maybe it will take us to the future!"

"Huh?" I had forgotten I had it in my hand.

"So thirsty . . ." Gwendolyn murmured, licking her dry lips. "So thirsty . . ."

I raised the *Vampire Breath* high. The blue glass bottle caught the light from the torch.

Gwendolyn gasped and drew back in fear.

I grabbed the top. And started to pull.

"No — please!" Gwendolyn begged. "Put that down! Don't open it! Please — don't open it!"

I squeezed the glass top — and pulled open the bottle.

23

Nothing happened.

All three of us stared at the open blue bottle in my hand.

"It takes a few seconds," I told Cara. My voice came out high and shaky. "Remember? Back in my basement, it took a few seconds. Then it came whooshing out."

Gwendolyn's eyes were wide, locked on the bottle.

We stared in tense silence.

A few seconds went by. Then a few more seconds.

Gwendolyn broke the silence with a gleeful laugh. "It's empty!" she declared through her laughter. "The castle is filled with empties! There's a whole room of them over there." She pointed into the darkness.

I raised the bottle to my face and squinted inside. Too dark to see anything. But Gwendolyn was right. It was definitely empty.

I let it fall to the floor.

Gwendolyn's grin was so evil in the shadowy light from the torch. I tried to back away. But I bumped into a stone column.

Trapped.

As she grinned so hungrily at me, Gwendolyn's fangs shone in the pale light. "So thirsty . . ." she whispered. "Freddy — don't run away. Help me. I'm so thirsty. . . ."

"*I'm thirsty, too!*" a voice boomed from behind me.

I spun around to see a flash of orange torchlight. The light bounced toward us. And inside it, I saw the angry face of Count Nightwing.

He floated to us, his eyes narrowed at Gwendolyn.

Her mouth dropped open. She raised both hands in front of her, as if to shield herself.

"Gwendolyn — what are you doing down here with *my* prisoners?" Count Nightwing demanded angrily.

He didn't give her a chance to reply. He floated up off the floor, floated over her. His cape floated out like bat wings. His silvery eyes locked on hers. And he opened his mouth in a furious hiss.

Gwendolyn's fangs glistened wetly in the torchlight. She tossed back her blond ringlets and, still shielding herself with both hands, hissed up at the old vampire.

Oh, wow! I thought. They're going to fight!

I leaned forward, horrified — but eager to watch.

The two vampires floated off the floor. They hissed at each other again, like two snakes about to strike.

"Freddy — come on!" Cara whispered. She grabbed my arm and pulled. "This is our chance."

Cara was right. While the two vampires hissed at each other, we had to try to get away.

My heart pounding, I grabbed Gwendolyn's torch off the floor and darted after Cara.

We ran blindly through the dark basement.

There's got to be a way out! I repeated to myself. There's *got* to be a way to escape!

Finally, I saw an open door.

Cara and I burst through the door. I glanced back. I saw Count Nightwing floating high off the floor. His cape swirled behind him. Gwendolyn hissed up at him weakly from the cellar floor.

No time to watch their fight. I followed Cara into the room. "Where are we?" I whispered.

I raised the torch in front of us.

"Wow," Cara murmured as the shelves against the wall came into the light. "I don't believe it!"

We had found the room of empty *Vampire Breath* bottles that Gwendolyn had told us about. Shelves covered every wall from floor to ceiling. And each shelf was crammed with blue bottles. Stacks and stacks of blue glass bottles.

“There must be a million empty bottles in here!” I whispered.

We gazed around the room. The bottles sparkled like blue jewels, caught in the light from the torch.

Cara shook her head hard, as if trying to shake the amazing sight from her eyes. She turned to me, her expression solemn. “This isn’t helping us escape,” she whispered.

“Escape?” a hoarse voice rasped from the doorway.

Count Nightwing moved quickly into the room. “There is no need to talk of escape,” he said, narrowing his strange silver eyes at Cara, then at me. “For there is no escape from Count Nightwing’s castle.”

He raised his cape and floated off the floor.

“What are you g-going to do?” I stammered.

He tossed back his bald head and uttered a frightening hiss.

I felt myself pushed back, back, deeper into the room. He was using some kind of force, some kind of ancient power.

He floated higher. The cape billowed around him. He looked like a frail insect inside a purple cocoon. But I could feel his power.

Pushing me back. . . . Holding me. . . . Pushing me. . . .

And then, suddenly, I felt him let go.

He dropped heavily to the floor. His eyes flashed. He snapped his bony fingers.

A thin-lipped smile creased his face. "Yesssss!" he hissed.

Cara and I backed up to the shelves at the far wall. My legs were trembling now. He had gripped me in some kind of ancient force. And now I felt totally shaky. I struggled to catch my breath.

"Yessss!" he hissed again. "I remember now!"

24

Cara and I stared at the old vampire in silence. He turned to the shelves of blue bottles.

"This is where I hid my full bottle of *Vampire Breath*," he told us. "I hid it here in the empties room. I knew the others would never look here."

As he smiled, I could see his gums, soft and smooth inside the dry-lipped mouth. His smile faded. And his silvery eyes narrowed.

"I'm so thirsty," he whispered, eyeing Cara and me. "I must find the full bottle — refresh my memory — and get back my fangs."

He dove for the nearest shelf and began pawing through the blue bottles. "Which one? Which one?" he muttered to himself. "Thousands of bottles, and only one is full."

His small, bony hands moved quickly over the shelf. He pushed aside empties, muttering to himself. Bottles crashed to the floor, shattering into pieces.

"Cara — quick!" I pointed to the far shelf. "Let's move!"

She understood me instantly. We had to find the full bottle first. We had to find it before Count Nightwing did.

I dropped to my knees and began sifting through the bottles on the bottom shelf. Empty . . . empty . . . empty . . . empty . . .

I pushed them aside one by one. My fingers moved quickly over the glass tops. I squinted hard in the dim light, searching, searching for the only full bottle.

Glass shattered on the hard floor. Bottles rolled and spun all around me.

Beside me, Cara worked frantically over a low shelf. "No. No. No. No." She muttered to herself as she moved her hands over the empty bottles.

"You two —" Count Nightwing called from across the room. "Get away from there!"

We ignored him. We kept pawing through the bottles, working faster, faster. Desperate to find the full one first.

And then — my hand landed on it.

I sucked in a deep breath when I realized it felt heavier than the others. My hand trembled as I carefully lifted it out from the others.

Yes! It definitely felt heavy. Yes! It was still sealed shut. Yes!

"I found it!" I cried, jumping to my feet. "Cara — look! I've got it!"

I raised the full bottle up to show it to her — and Count Nightwing grabbed it from my hand.

"Thank you," he said.

25

With an eager smile, the old vampire raised the bottle and reached to open it.

"Noooo!" I howled.

I leaped at him. Caught him by surprise.

I shoved my shoulder into his chest. He felt light and feathery, as if he had no bones at all.

He uttered a startled choking sound.

The bottle of *Vampire Breath* flew from his hand.

I reached out — and grabbed it in the air.

Holding it tightly in both hands, I backed toward the shelves.

Count Nightwing recovered quickly. He narrowed his eyes at me, and once again, I felt his strange power holding me, holding me in place.

"Freddy, you will hand the bottle to me now," he ordered in a soft, calm voice.

I didn't move. I couldn't.

"Hand the bottle to me now," the old vampire

insisted, floating toward me, his bony hand outstretched. "You will hand it to me, Freddy."

I swallowed hard. I couldn't give him the *Vampire Breath.* I knew that Cara and I were doomed if Count Nightwing opened it.

But I couldn't move. He had frozen me there. I was helpless!

"Hand it to me," he insisted. He reached for the bottle.

"Monkey in the Middle!" I heard Cara call.

She seemed far away. And at first, her words didn't make any sense to me.

"Monkey in the Middle!" she called again.

This time, I understood.

I sucked in a deep breath. It took all my strength to move my arm.

Count Nightwing swiped at the bottle. His bony fingertips brushed against it.

But I tossed the bottle high over his shoulder.

Cara bobbled it, fumbled it into the air — and then grabbed it. "The catch of the day!" she cried.

With an angry groan, Count Nightwing spun around. "Give me that!" he rasped. He dove toward Cara.

She pulled her arm back and heaved the bottle to me. A low toss which zipped past the old vampire's knees. I caught it at my shoelaces.

Count Nightwing whirled back to me. His strange eyes narrowed in fury. "I want that bottle!" he snarled.

I tossed it high, over his head. Cara caught it in one hand.

When we baby-sat for Tyler Brown, Cara and I played Monkey in the Middle all the time. That little shrimp could never take the ball away from us. We could keep him running back and forth for hours!

But I knew Count Nightwing would soon run out of patience. There was no way Cara and I could win this game.

But what else could we do?

The old vampire dove for Cara, his hands outstretched, his cape flying.

Cara tossed off-balance. I stretched for the bottle. But it sailed past my open hand.

And crashed into a shelf.

Bottles toppled and broke.

Count Nightwing flew to the shelf. He grabbed blindly at the bottles.

But I got there first. I picked up the bottle and tossed it to Cara.

"No — !" Count Nightwing rasped. "Enough!"

He hurtled toward Cara.

She tossed the bottle to me, a high throw over the old vampire's head.

I raised my hands to catch it.

But to my surprise, Count Nightwing flew straight up — and caught the bottle in both hands.

As he sailed slowly back to the floor, a pleased

smile spread over his face. "I win," he said softly, his eyes flashing. "I win. It helps to be able to fly."

He raised the bottle in front of him.

"No — don't!" I begged.

His smile grew even wider. He reached out — and pulled the top off the bottle.

26

All three of us froze. And stared at the open bottle in Count Nightwing's hand.

"No," Cara murmured. "No — please."

A few seconds passed. A few more seconds.

"Nothing is happening," Count Nightwing whispered. His smile faded. He raised the bottle to his face and tilted it to see inside.

Beneath the purple cape, his slender shoulders slumped. He sighed, a long, dry sigh. "Empty," he said. "This bottle is empty, too."

Cara and I exchanged glances. I suddenly knew what had happened. In my wild scramble to pick up the bottle, I had grabbed the wrong one off the shelf.

Sure enough. I turned to the shelf — and spotted the full bottle right in front of me.

"I have it!" I cried. I picked it up carefully from the shelf. "I have it!"

The old vampire let out a furious growl. He leaped at me.

"Cara — catch!" I screamed.

I heaved the bottle to her.

But Count Nightwing swung his arm. His hand slapped the bottle in midair.

"Oh — !" I gasped as the bottle sailed into the wall.

It bounced off. Crashed to the floor. Cracked open.

And the sour, dark mist poured up into the room.

"We've lost," I murmured. "We're doomed."

27

I tried to hold my breath, but it didn't help. The foul odor of the rising fog seemed to seep into my skin.

Across the room, I saw Cara cup a hand tightly over her nose and mouth. Her dark eyes grew wide in fright. She waved her other hand frantically, trying to fan the smelly fog away from her.

I choked on it. My eyes started to burn. I closed them. Felt hot tears seep down my cheeks.

When I opened my eyes, I couldn't see Cara anymore. The fog had grown too thick.

I could see Count Nightwing's purple cape, dark inside the mist. Then it disappeared, too.

And I was alone. Alone inside a thick, billowing cloud.

I dropped to my knees. Covered my face with

both hands. I tried not to breathe. I could taste the foul mist on my tongue!

How long did I kneel there? I'm not sure.

But when I finally opened my burning eyes, the fog was fading.

Count Nightwing's purple cape came back into view as the mist lowered itself to the floor. And I saw Cara across the room, shielding her face with one arm.

The fog continued to melt away.

The room came back into focus.

And I realized I was staring at an air hockey game.

I blinked several times. A pool table stood in the center of the room.

Pool table? Air hockey?

Cara came running over to me, her dark eyes flashing with excitement. "We're back, Freddy!" she cried happily. "We're back in your basement!"

"Yesssss!" I cheered. I pumped both fists in the air. "Yessss!"

I staggered across the room and hugged the air hockey game. Then I kissed the wall. I actually kissed the wall!

"We're back! We're back!" Cara chanted, jumping up and down. "The *Vampire Breath* — it brought us back to your house, Freddy!"

"Noooooo!"

I turned to see Count Nightwing toss back his head in a long, angry wail. He swirled his cape behind him, then clasped his hands into tight fists.

"Noooooo! Noooooo! This can't be happening!" he cried hoarsely.

Cara and I huddled together as the vampire advanced on us.

"I don't want to be here!" he declared. "I must go back. I must find my fangs! Without my fangs, I will not survive. I will perish!"

He rose up over us. His eyes burned angrily down at us. His dry lips quivered. He stretched out his cape as if to trap us inside it.

"I must go back!" he rasped. "Where is the *Vampire Breath*? Where is the blue bottle?"

My eyes glanced quickly around the room.

No sign of it.

"It didn't come back with us," Cara announced.

The old vampire tossed back his head in another angry wail.

Then, raising his cape even higher, he swooped down to attack us.

Cara and I staggered back against the pool table.

The vampire moved quickly, wrapping his heavy, purple cape around us both.

We were trapped. Nowhere to move.

Then, suddenly, the cape slid off. Count Nightwing took a step back. His mouth dropped open in surprise.

I followed his gaze — and saw Mom and Dad hurrying into the basement. "Mom!" I cried. "Dad! Look out! He's a vampire! He's a real vampire!"

28

Count Nightwing squinted at my parents, his mouth still open in shock. He locked his stare on my mom. "Cynthia — ?" he cried. "Cynthia, what are *you* doing here?"

Mom smiled at him. "Daddy, you finally woke up!" she exclaimed.

"Huh?" Cara and I both gasped in shock.

Mom rushed forward and threw her arms around the old vampire. She hugged him for a long time.

"Daddy, you've been napping down here for at least a hundred years," she said. "We didn't know whether to wake you or let you sleep."

Dad came rushing over, too, a big smile on his face. He rested a hand on my shoulder. "Did you meet our son Freddy?" he asked Count Nightwing. "This is Freddy — your grandson."

Grandson?

Me?

I'm the vampire's grandson?

Count Nightwing stared down at me, shaking his head. I could see that he was as confused as I was!

"Cynthia — ?" he said to my mom. "Cynthia — my fangs. I've lost my fangs."

Mom slid her arm around the vampire's waist. "Daddy, your fangs aren't lost," she told him. "They're in the glass in the bathroom. Right where you left them."

"Here. Over here," Dad said. He led the way to the little bathroom in the corner that we never use.

A few seconds later, Count Nightwing stepped out, adjusting the fangs over his gums with both of his thumbs. "There. That's better," he said. "Now let's fly out of here. I'm so thirsty! It's been a hundred years!"

Mom and Dad turned to me. "We'll be home soon," Dad said. "Make yourself a sandwich upstairs, okay? Make one for Cara, too."

I stared back at him, unable to get over my shock. "But if you and Mom are vampires, am I a vampire, too?" I asked in a trembling voice.

"Of course," Mom replied. "But you're way too young to get your fangs, Freddy. You have to wait at least another hundred years!"

I wanted to ask a million more questions. But the three of them began to flap their arms. Up and down. In seconds, they changed into bats and flew out the basement window.

I stared at the window for a long while, trying to calm down, trying to slow my racing heart. When I started to feel a little more normal, I turned to Cara.

"Wow," she said, shaking her head. "Wow."

"I don't believe it, either," I replied softly.

She grinned at me. "I knew you were weird, Freddy. But I didn't know you were *that* weird!"

I wanted to laugh at that. But I was still too shocked to laugh, or cry, or scream — or do anything!

I turned away from Cara and counted to twenty, trying to get myself together.

It isn't easy to find out that you're a vampire.

I really think Mom and Dad could have broken the news to me in a little better way.

But I guess they didn't think it was any big deal . . .

The door to the bathroom stood open. I stepped inside. "We never use this bathroom," I muttered. "We use the one across the basement."

Cara followed me in. The mirrored door to the medicine chest was partly open. She pulled it open the rest of the way.

The shelves were jammed with all kinds of jars and bottles. Strange medicines and tubes of ointments.

I saw a green glass bottle on the top shelf. "What's that?" I wondered. I stretched my hand up to pull it down.

But Cara grabbed it first.

"Give it back!" I cried. I shoved her.

She shoved me back.

She turned the glass bottle in her hand and read the name on the label to me: "*WEREWOLF SWEAT.*"

"Cara — put it back!" I ordered. "No. Really. Put it back. Leave it alone, Cara. Don't open it. Don't —"

She teased me. Grinning, she pretended to pull off the top.

"No — !" I cried.

I swiped at it. Tried to pull it from her hand.

But I missed — and tugged off the top instead.

"Whooooa!" Cara cried out as a yellow liquid squirted over both of us.

I rolled my eyes. "*Now* what?" I cried. "*Now* what do you think is going to happen?"

"*Grrrrrrrowwwwwrrrrrrrr!*" Cara replied.

ABOUT R. L. STINE

R. L. Stine is the most popular author in America. He is the creator of the *Goosebumps, Give Yourself Goosebumps, Fear Street,* and *Ghosts of Fear Street* series among other popular books. He has written more than 100 scary novels for kids.

Bob lives in New York with his wife, Jane, and teenage son, Matt.

Add *more*

Goosebumps®

to your collection . . .
A chilling preview of
what's next from
R.L. STINE

CALLING ALL CREEPS

12

I fumbled for the phone in the dark. Knocked it off the bedtable. It clattered loudly onto the floor.

I dove out of bed and grabbed the receiver. Then I hunched on my knees, listening for Mom and Dad. Did they hear the phone ring? I'm not allowed to get calls after ten o'clock.

I cleared my throat and raised the phone to my ear. "Hello?"

"Ricky — it's me. Iris."

I glanced at my clock radio. "Iris? It's midnight. How come you're calling so late?" I asked. "Are you okay?"

"My father was on the phone practically the whole night. Ricky — did you see the school paper?" she demanded in an urgent whisper.

"Huh? No," I replied, climbing onto the edge of my bed. "When they started to pass out the newspapers, I got called to the library. The librarian wanted to ask me about a bunch of books

I lost. When I came back to the room, all the papers were gone."

"So you didn't see the paper?" Iris asked shrilly.

"No," I repeated. "I didn't get my copy. Is it great? Can you read the message at the bottom okay?"

"Well . . ." Iris hesitated.

"Is it great?" I asked excitedly.

"Not exactly," Iris replied softly. "Actually, Ricky, you're in . . . major trouble."

"I'm what?" I squeezed the phone to my ear. She was talking so softly, I could barely hear her. "Iris . . . I'm *what*?"

"In major trouble," she repeated.

A chill swept down my back. "Major trouble? But — why, Iris? What do you m-mean?" I sputtered.

"The message —" she started.

Then she stopped. Silence on the other end.

"Iris — I can't hear you!" I said. "Iris — ?"

"Uh oh," she murmured. "I've got to get off. My dad is screaming at me."

"But, Iris —" I insisted. "Why am I in trouble? You've *got* to tell me!"

"*I'm getting off!*" I heard her call to her father. "*It was only a short call, Dad. I know it's midnight!*"

"Iris, please — tell me. Tell me before you hang up!" I begged.

"Got to go. Bye," she said. I heard a click. The line went dead.

I slammed the receiver down angrily. What was her problem? Why couldn't she tell my why I was in trouble?

I slid the phone back in place beside the clock radio and climbed into bed. I punched my pillow a few times, puffing it up. Then I pulled the blankets up to my chin.

I shut my eyes and tried to calm down enough to fall asleep.

The phone rang again.

I sat straight up with a startled gasp. This time I managed to pick up the phone without knocking it to the floor.

"Iris, thanks for calling me back," I whispered.

"I saw your message in the school newspaper," a voice whispered.

"Iris — ?" I swallowed hard. I knew it wasn't Iris.

"I saw your message," the voice whispered. "I am calling as you instructed."

"Huh? You're calling *me*?" I cried.

"Yes. I'm following your instructions," came the whispered reply.

"Hey — who *is* this?" I demanded.

"I'm a Creep."

13

I slammed down the phone.

Then I settled back into my bed. I puffed up my pillows again, and pulled the blanket over my shoulders.

The wind howled outside my bedroom window. Shadows cast by the streetlamp in front of our house danced over my wall.

My brain was spinning.

Who *was* that?

I couldn't be sure, but it sounded like a boy. Why did he call *me*? The message I put in the newspaper gave *Tasha's* phone number.

I didn't have long to think about it. The phone rang again.

I grabbed up the receiver before the first ring ended. My eyes shot to the bedroom door. If Mom or Dad heard me getting these calls, I'd *really* be in major trouble!

"Hello? Who is it?" I demanded.

"Hi. I'm a Creep." A different voice. A boy. Speaking softly.

"Huh?" I gasped.

"I'm a Creep. I called as soon as I saw your orders."

"Give me a break!" I cried. I slammed down the phone.

"What is going on?" I muttered out loud. I sat staring at the phone. Watching it in the dim light. Waiting.

Was it going to ring again?

"Ricky — !" a voice boomed.

I jumped a mile.

The ceiling light clicked on. Dad stood in the doorway in his blue-and-white striped pajamas. He scratched his cheek. "Ricky — what are all those calls about?" he demanded.

I shrugged. "Calls?"

He narrowed his eyes at me suspiciously. "I heard the phone ring three times," he growled.

"Oh. You mean *those* calls!" I tried to sound innocent. But I knew I didn't stand a chance.

"You know you're not allowed to get calls after ten," Dad said sharply. He yawned. "It is after midnight. Now *who* is calling so late?"

"It's some kind of a joke," I told him. "You know. Kids from school."

He brushed his sandy hair off his forehead. "I don't think it's funny," he said.

I lowered my head. "I know. But it isn't my fault —"

He raised a hand to silence me. "Tell your friends to stop," he said. "I mean it. If they keep calling so late, I'll have to take your phone away."

"I'll tell them," I promised.

I'd tell them to stop, I thought, *if I knew who they were!*

Dad yawned again. He has the loudest yawn in the world. It sounds more like a roar.

When he finished yawning, he clicked off the light and disappeared back to his room.

As soon as he left, the phone rang again.

"Please —" I started.

"I'm a Creep," a whispered voice told me. A girl this time. "I saw your message. I'm ready. Ready to plant. Ready to rule. When will the Creeps meet?"

"Huh? Meet?" I didn't wait for an answer. I hung up the phone.

Staring at the phone, I felt totally confused.

Why am *I* getting all these calls? I wondered.

Is there some kind of a mix-up?

And why are the calls so strange? Why did that girl say she's ready to plant? Ready to rule?

What is going on?

The phone rang again . . .

14

The next morning, I dragged myself to school. The phone hadn't stopped ringing until two in the morning. That's when I took it off the hook. I spent the rest of the night, twisting and turning, thinking about all the weird calls.

I didn't fall asleep until seven. Which is the time my alarm goes off to wake me up!

At breakfast, my head nearly dropped into my corn flakes. I just wanted to go back to bed. But Mom and Dad didn't feel sorry for me at all.

They were furious. The ringing phone had kept them awake too.

"You tell those kids not to call again," Mom warned. "Or else I'll go in to your school and tell them myself!"

"No — please!" I begged. "I'll tell them. I'll tell them this morning! They won't call again. I promise!"

Can you think of anything more embarrassing than having your mom come to school, barge into your classroom, and lecture the kids in your class?

They already make fun of me every day and call me "Sicky Ricky." Can you *imagine* what they would call me if my mom came to school and yelled at them all?

Whoa!

Just thinking about it gave me icy chills.

It took all my strength to pull myself to school and slump through the crowded hall to my locker.

"There you are!" Iris cried.

I saw her waiting across from my locker. She wore a loose plaid shirt over navy blue corduroy pants. Her long, plastic earrings jangled softly.

She had been leaning against the tile wall. Now she pushed through a group of girls to get to me. "Here, Ricky. Take a look."

She handed me yesterday's copy of the *Harding Herald*. I grabbed it eagerly and lowered my eyes to the bottom of the front page.

Yes. There it was. In tiny type across the whole bottom margin. My message.

Except it had been changed a little.

I moved my lips, reading it softly to myself:

"*Calling all Creeps. Calling all Creeps. If you're a real Creep, call Ricky after midnight.*" Then it gave my phone number.

My phone number. Not Tasha's.

My name and number.

I let out a low moan and weakly handed the paper back to Iris.

She shook her head and tsk-tsked. "You look terrible. Did you get any sleep at all?" she asked.

"No," I murmured.

I grabbed the newspaper back and read it again. "How did this happen?" I cried.

Tasha's grinning face flashed into my mind.

"Tasha!" I screamed her name. And then I took off, pushing my way through groups of kids, hurtling over someone's backpack.

I ran down the long, curving hall to the eighth-grade classrooms. And burst into Tasha's room just as the early bell rang.

My eyes frantically swept the room. I spotted her near the front, handing a notebook to another girl.

"Tasha —" I called running up to her. I waved the newspaper in her face. "I — I —" I sputtered breathlessly.

She tossed back her red curls and laughed. "I caught your little joke just in time," she said. "Did you get any calls last night, Ricky?"

"A few," I muttered angrily.

The whole class burst out laughing at me. Even the teacher.

All morning, I had the feeling that everyone was watching me. Laughing at me.

Maybe I imagined it. Maybe I didn't.

I kept thinking about the calls I'd received the night before. I knew they were all from kids at school. But why were they saying such strange things?

"I saw your instructions . . ."

"I'm ready to plant. Ready to rule."

"When will the Creeps meet?"

At lunch, I carried my tray toward the corner in back of the lunchroom. I didn't feel like eating with anyone. I didn't feel like hearing more jokes, more kids laughing at me.

I had to walk past the table where my four seventh-grade enemies always sat.

Uh-oh, I thought. Wart and David were squirting their mile cartons at each other. Brenda laughed so hard, chocolate milk ran out of her nose.

They see me. I'm going to get a milk shower, I realized. Too late to go the other way.

To my shock, I passed right by the table without getting splashed or hit by anything. Wart didn't call out any nasty jokes. David and Jared didn't try to trip me.

What's going on? I wondered as I hurried to the far corner of the room. I know they saw me.

Why didn't they chant "Sicky Ricky" and toss their drink cartons at me the way they always do? They let me pass by as if they didn't know me.

I slid my tray across the back table. No one ever sits in this corner. It's next to the furnace duct. Hot air blows out over the table while you eat.

I had picked up a sandwich of some kind of lunchmeat and a bowl of tomato soup. I tilted my chair back against the wall and sat chewing on the sandwich, watching the other kids.

Waiting. Waiting for someone to come over and make a joke about how my tomato soup looked like clotted blood. Or make a joke about all the calls I got after midnight.

Waiting for kids to start chanting "Sicky Ricky." Or for Wart or one of my other pals at his table to start throwing food at me.

But no.

No one paid any attention to me. I leaned back and ate my lunch in peace.

I finished the soup and half the sandwich. I had picked up a bowl of chocolate pudding for dessert. But the crust was too thick to force my spoon through.

I gathered up my tray and stood up to leave.

And someone hit me in the forehead with a wadded-up piece of paper.

"Hey — !" I called out angrily. But secretly, I felt glad. I mean, I just didn't feel normal going a whole lunch hour without anyone getting on my case.

Rubbing my forehead, I glanced down at the paper. And realized it had writing on it. A note. Someone had passed me a note.

I unfolded it and quickly read the scribbled words:

When will the Creeps meet?

GET Goosebumps®

by R.L. Stine

❑ BAB45365-3	#1	Welcome to Dead House	$3.99
❑ BAB45366-1	#2	Stay Out of the Basement	$3.99
❑ BAB45367-X	#3	Monster Blood	$3.99
❑ BAB45368-8	#4	Say Cheese and Die!	$3.99
❑ BAB45369-6	#5	The Curse of the Mummy's Tomb	$3.99
❑ BAB49445-7	#10	The Ghost Next Door	$3.99
❑ BAB49450-3	#15	You Can't Scare Me!	$3.99
❑ BAB47742-0	#20	The Scarecrow Walks at Midnight	$3.99
❑ BAB47743-9	#21	Go Eat Worms!	$3.99
❑ BAB47744-7	#22	Ghost Beach	$3.99
❑ BAB47745-5	#23	Return of the Mummy	$3.99
❑ BAB48354-4	#24	Phantom of the Auditorium	$3.99
❑ BAB48355-2	#25	Attack of the Mutant	$3.99
❑ BAB48350-1	#26	My Hairiest Adventure	$3.99
❑ BAB48351-X	#27	A Night in Terror Tower	$3.99
❑ BAB48352-8	#28	The Cuckoo Clock of Doom	$3.99
❑ BAB48347-1	#29	Monster Blood III	$3.99
❑ BAB48348-X	#30	It Came from Beneath the Sink	$3.99
❑ BAB48349-8	#31	The Night of the Living Dummy II	$3.99
❑ BAB48344-7	#32	The Barking Ghost	$3.99
❑ BAB48345-5	#33	The Horror at Camp Jellyjam	$3.99
❑ BAB48346-3	#34	Revenge of the Lawn Gnomes	$3.99
❑ BAB48340-4	#35	A Shocker on Shock Street	$3.99
❑ BAB56873-6	#36	The Haunted Mask II	$3.99
❑ BAB56874-4	#37	The Headless Ghost	$3.99
❑ BAB56875-2	#38	The Abominable Snowman of Pasadena	$3.99
❑ BAB56876-0	#39	How I Got My Shrunken Head	$3.99
❑ BAB56877-9	#40	Night of the Living Dummy III	$3.99
❑ BAB56878-7	#41	Bad Hare Day	$3.99
❑ BAB56879-5	#42	Egg Monsters from Mars	$3.99
❑ BAB56880-9	#43	The Beast from the East	$3.99
❑ BAB56881-7	#44	Say Cheese and Die–Again!	$3.99
❑ BAB56882-5	#45	Ghost Camp	$3.99
❑ BAB56883-3	#46	How to Kill a Monster	$3.99
❑ BAB56884-1	#47	Legend of the Lost Legend	$3.99
❑ BAB56885-X	#48	Attack of the Jack-O'-Lanterns	$3.99
❑ BAB56886-8	#49	Vampire Breath	$3.99

GOOSEBUMPS PRESENTS

❑ BAB74586-7	Goosebumps Presents TV Episode #1 The Girl Who Cried Monster	$3.99
❑ BAB74587-5	Goosebumps Presents TV Episode #2 The Cuckoo Clock of Doom	$3.99
❑ BAB74588-3	Goosebumps Presents TV Episode #3 Welcome to Camp Nightmare	$3.99
❑ BAB74589-1	Goosebumps Presents TV Episode #4 Return of the Mummy	$3.99
❑ BAB74590-5	Goosebumps Presents TV Episode #5 Night of the Living Dummy II	$3.99

Curly's All-New and Shocking
Goosebumps®
Fan Club Pack
Only $8.95
Plus $2.00 shipping and handling*
CURLY
Zipper tag
Glow-in-the-Dark Pen
Folder
THE OFFICIAL Goosebumps FAN CLUB
Game sheets
Wallet
Goosebumps
Shipping box
HERE LIES Goosebumps THE OFFICIAL GOOSEBUMPS FAN CLUB
Notepad
Curly Bio
THE OFFICIAL Goosebumps FAN CLUB
CURLY
Unboo-lievable, dudes!
It's more exclusive, new
Goosebumps stuff to collect!
Get the inside scary scoop on
the latest books, the TV show, videos,
games—and everything Goosebumps!
All this plus:
• Game sheets
• Notepad
• Sticker
• A subscription to the official newsletter, The Scream
(mailed separately—a few weeks after you receive your pack)
To get your all-new Goosebumps Fan Club Pack (in the U.S. and Canada only), just fill out the coupon below and send it with your check or money order. U.S. residents: $8.95 plus $2.00 shipping and handling to Goosebumps Fan Club, Scholastic Inc., P.O. Box 7500, 2931 East McCarty Street, Jefferson City, MO 65102. Canadian residents: $13.95 plus $2.00 shipping and handling to Goosebumps Fan Club, Scholastic Canada, 123 Newkirk Road, Richmond Hill, Ontario, L4C3G5. Offer expires 9/30/97. Offer good for one year from date of receipt. Please allow 4-6 weeks for your introductory pack to arrive.
*Canadian prices slightly higher. Fan club offer expires 9/30/97. Membership good for one year from date of receipt. Newsletters sent four times during membership.
Hurry! Send me my all-new Goosebumps Fan Club Pack. I am enclosing my check or money order (no cash please) for U.S. residents: $10.95 ($8.95 plus $2.00) and for Canadian residents: $15.95 ($13.95 plus $2.00).
Name ____ Birthdate ____
Address ____
City ____ State ____ Zip ____
Telephone ( ) ____ Boy ____ Girl ____
Where did you buy this book? ❑ Bookstore ❑ Book Fair ❑ Book Club ❑ Other
© 1996 Parachute Press, Inc. GOOSEBUMPS is a registered trademark of Parachute Press, Inc. All Rights Reserved.
GBFC396